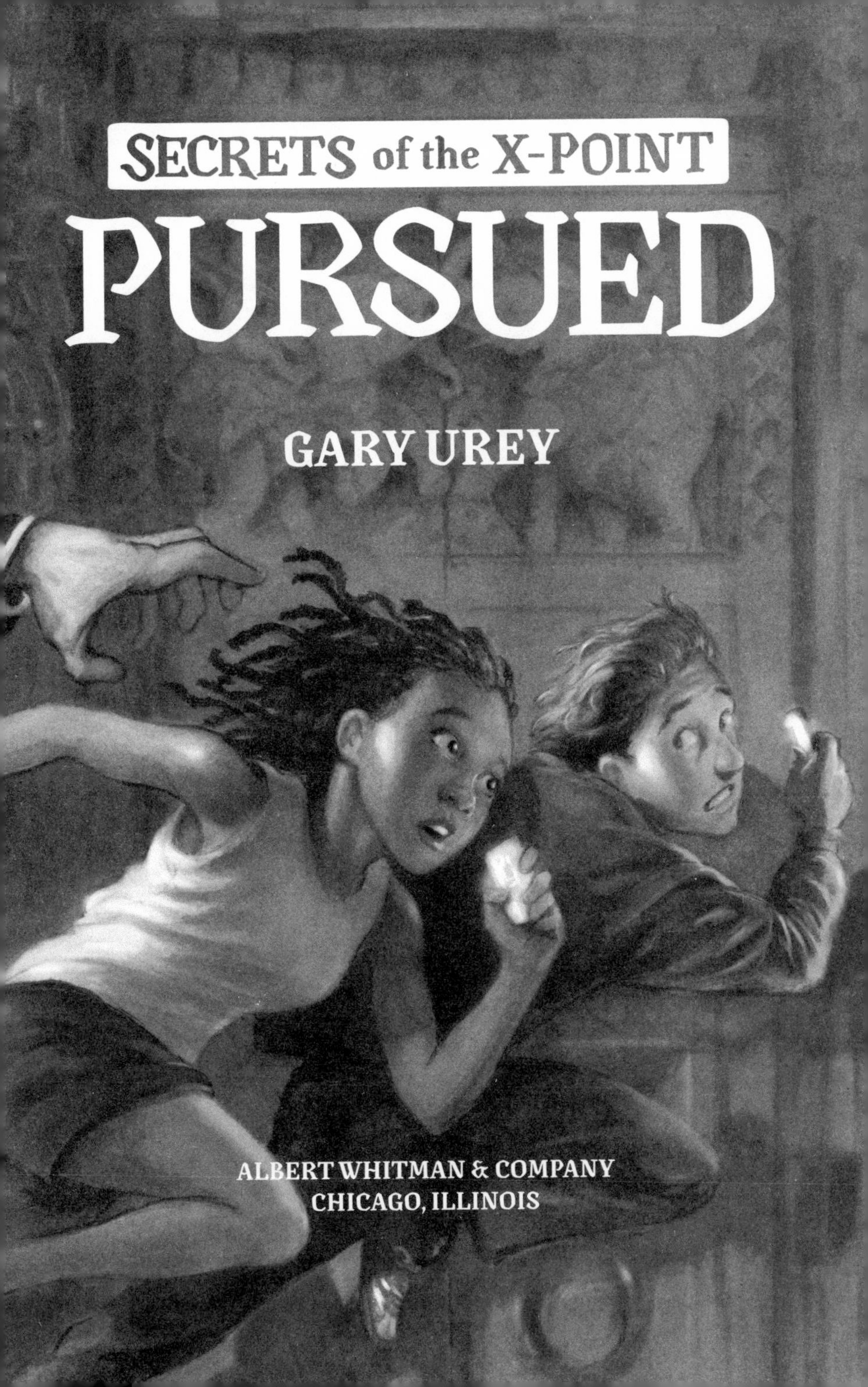

SECRETS of the X-POINT

PURSUED

GARY UREY

ALBERT WHITMAN & COMPANY
CHICAGO, ILLINOIS

For Melissa

Library of Congress Cataloging-in-Publication
data is on file with the publisher.

Published in 2017 by Albert Whitman & Company
ISBN 978-0-8075-6684-8 (hardcover)
ISBN 978-0-8075-6686-2 (paperback)

Printed in the United States of America
10 9 8 7 6 5 4 3 2 1 BP 20 19 18 17 16

Design by Jordan Kost

For more information about Albert Whitman & Company,
visit our website at www.albertwhitman.com.

Chapter One
AXEL

Axel Jack exploded out of thin air and hit the concrete with a bone-crunching thud.

His head throbbed, and his body ached from the sudden blast through the Satellite Warp. He shook off the impact, lifted his head, and saw the shoes of passing pedestrians—sneakers, high heels, loafers, wing tips, sandals. A set of dirty bare feet walked directly toward him.

"You Houdini?" a grizzled voice asked.

A gnarled, arthritic finger touched Axel's shoulder.

Axel clutched the GeoPort unit in his jeans pocket and sat up on his knees, every muscle tensed to run. The old guy towering over him had a long beard and a pockmarked face, and smelled like he'd just urinated all over himself. Relief swelled in Axel's chest. The man definitely wasn't a Pursuer. He was safe—for the moment.

He stood up and stared at the strange surroundings. Hundreds of people clogged the busy sidewalks. Honking yellow taxis whizzed down the street. Skyscrapers soared into the clouds like giant man-made mountains.

"I'm in a city," Axel said. "A big freaking city."

"New York City," the man mumbled. "You a magician or something?"

"Huh?" Axel grunted back.

"One minute I'm drooling over a sweet hunk of carrot cake in that deli window, and the next I see you. A loud boom like a car backfiring and then a big puff of smoke like you was in a magic show or something."

"I wish it were magic. You said I'm in New York City, right?"

"The one and only Big Apple. Got a dollar?"

Axel reached into his pocket and pulled out a bill. "Here you go. Sorry, it's Vietnamese dong. That's where I just came from." He hoisted his backpack over his shoulders and sprinted down the street.

The weather was warm, but not like the oppressive humidity of Vietnam where his last chase had taken place. He took off his jacket, tied it around his waist, and headed toward a patch of green in the otherwise gray urban landscape. The GeoPort vibrated in his pocket.

He quickly took the palm-sized, twenty-first-century version of the Holy Grail out and read the coordinates.

40.7420° N, 73.9876° W

"Madison Square Park," Axel said aloud. "Homeless people never lie. I'm smack-dab in the heart of New York City."

Axel slipped the GeoPort back into his pocket, his eyes nervously scanning the faces in the crowd. He knew the Pursuers back in Vietnam had a short window of opportunity to find the Warp with their trackers. If they sniffed it out, some extremely nasty men would soon materialize in front of the deli with the carrot cake in the window.

A bright yellow sun beamed high in the sky. Axel knew from the sun's position that it was noon on a hot June day. If the Pursuers were able to follow him, he'd have to run and hide for the next nine hours or so. Until the sun went down and the Pursuers' solar tracking device could no longer pinpoint his location. He grabbed a spare shirt from his backpack, wiped the sweat off his flushed face, and jogged down the street.

One thought raced through his mind as he dashed in and out of the throngs of walkers choking the sidewalks: Daisha, her look of surprise and shocked horror when the Pursuers had burst into the Café Gac

Hoa at 92 Pham Ngoc Thach in District Three of Ho Chi Minh City.

Their peaceful, relaxing lunch of spring rolls and iced tea had suddenly exploded into glass breaking, tables overturning, and angry shouts in the dialect of the Pursuers. The chaos was so intense that he and Daisha hadn't had time to synchronize their GeoPorts. All Axel remembered was frantically pushing buttons, blindly setting new coordinates on their GeoPorts, and then disappearing into the temporary safety of the Warp.

Moments later, the Warp dumped him on a street in New York City and Daisha was...

He had no idea because he hadn't seen her coordinates on the GeoPort. She could be in Spain, Alaska, Tel Aviv, or Timbuktu.

A loud groan came from the pit of his stomach. The Pursuers had ruined his lunch in the Ho Chi Minh City café. He scrounged around in his backpack for money. Besides the forty-two thousand in Vietnamese dong, equaling about two US dollars, he had a handful of change in US currency. The beefy scent of hot dogs drifted inside his nostrils. He crossed the busy street and ordered one from a place called the Dog House.

"Three fifty," said the man behind the cash register.

Axel dumped his change on the counter. "I have

three dollars and five cents," he said.

"Dog is three fifty. Better come up with another forty-five cents."

As Axel was scraping away his change, a woman with dyed purple hair shouted from behind him. "Just give the kid a hot dog," she said. "I'll cover him."

The man shrugged and handed Axel a hot dog. He was just about to douse his lunch with mustard when he saw two very familiar-looking men standing on the opposite corner of the street. One was tall and muscular. The other was slightly shorter and heavier but just as athletic looking. Both wore their short blond hair in a military cut. They had on black pants and matching black suit jackets with white shirts.

The taller of the two men pulled a round electronic device the size of an Oreo cookie from his pocket. He pointed it toward the Dog House. The GeoPort in Axel's pocket throbbed to life, buzzing and vibrating like an angry wasp trapped under a glass.

The Pursuers had found him.

The chase was on.

Chapter Two
DAISHA

Daisha Tandala landed face-first in the dirt. She let out a loud groan and checked her extremities for injury. Besides a dizzy head and nauseous stomach from her sudden plunge into the Satellite Warp, she felt okay. She stood up, wiped the grime and muck from her face, and scanned her location. She was right in the middle of a flowing sea of green.

"I'm in a huge field of corn," she mumbled.

The sunny June sky above her head was bright blue and cloudless. That meant if the Pursuers back in Vietnam had found their opening, they would burst through the Warp exactly where she had fallen moments ago. And they'd have lots of sunshine for their solar trackers. She reached into her pocket, pulled out her palm-sized GeoPort, and read the coordinates.

40.4150° N, 82.4603° W

"I have no idea where I am," she growled.

Thick woods surrounded the perimeter of the cornfield. She grabbed her new satchel off the ground—the one Axel had bought for her at the Binh Tay Market—and made a dash toward the trees. Her arms pumped furiously; her strong legs powered her between the rows of corn.

A dog barked behind her. A voice called out, "Who the heck are you?"

She stopped running and saw a big, black mutt with a white spot on its chest and a scruffy boy no older than eight or nine emerge from a row of corn.

"This is my dad's farm," the boy said. "What are you doing here?"

"Where am I?" Daisha asked.

"I told you...It's my dad's farm. Well, really it's my grandpa's farm, but it'll be ours when he croaks."

"No. I mean what part of the country. You speak English just like me so I'm assuming it's the United States."

The boy and the dog cocked their heads and gave her a confused look. "Ohio," he said. "Don't you even know where you are?"

Daisha looked past the boy to where she had landed in the cornfield. "Some days I do," she said with a shaky voice. "Some days I don't."

“Did you hear the thunder and see that smoke?” the boy asked, stroking the dog’s head. “It scared Moxie here half to death, and there ain’t a rain cloud in the sky.”

She couldn’t tell the boy what he had really heard and seen: a sonic boom caused by a very frightened girl hurtling through the Warp faster than the speed of sound. The smoke was from the massive discharge of electrical energy.

“You have funny hair,” the boy said.

“What do you mean *funny*?” Daisha asked.

“Looks like you haven’t washed it in a year.”

“For your information, they’re called dreadlocks. I’m half Jamaican and half Kenyan.” She threw up her hands in exasperation. “I don’t have time for this. What town am I near?”

“Mount Vernon. Fredericktown is farther down the road.”

“How far away is Mount Vernon?”

“About a mile.” The boy pointed east into the trees. “You can get to town by going that way. A path through the woods leads to a creek. There’s a fallen tree over the creek, and you can walk across it like a bridge. The path leads to the water park. The town center isn't far from there. How old are you?”

“Thirteen,” Daisha said. “Thanks for the information.

If you run into some strange men, don't tell them you saw me."

"What strange men?" the boy asked.

Daisha didn't answer him. She turned and started running toward the woods in the direction of the path.

The cornfield seemed to stretch forever, the trees like a mirage in the distance. A tiny part of Daisha was glad Axel wasn't with her this time. She was a much faster runner than he was. He would have just slowed her down, making their odds of capture that much greater. But what Axel Jack lacked in foot speed, he more than made up for in brainpower. The kid was hella smart and an expert at fooling the Pursuers.

A loud rumbling sound stopped Daisha in her tracks. She quickly hit the ground, lowering her head below the silky tassels of corn. The sound had come from the exact spot where she had burst through the Warp. A thick plume of smoke rose over the field.

"They're here," she whispered under her breath.

Daisha peeked over the tops of the cornstalks, and her heart nearly exploded in her chest. She could see two men walking in her direction. They were dressed in black suits with white shirts. The taller of the two men reached into his pocket and pulled out a round electronic device. Daisha knew instantly that it was a solar tracker. The man scanned the cornfield and then pointed the tracker in her direction. The GeoPort vibrated in her pocket.

The two men smiled and then slapped a high five.

The Pursuers had found her.

Chapter Three
DOCTOR STAIN

Doctor Lennon Hatch stared at the two giant monitors with the intensity of a fox ready to pounce on an unsuspecting mouse.

"The boy has a chance in the city," the Doctor said. "But the girl is as good as ours in the middle of an Ohio cornfield."

"Don't be so sure," said Pinchole, the Doctor's DSWS—director of Satellite Warp science. "But at least we've got them separated this time."

"Yes. Our men in Vietnam did a masterful job of surprising them in that café."

Each monitor was a high-resolution, incredibly detailed topographical satellite map. Three fast-moving blips on each kept the Doctor's eyes fixed to the screens. Two deep red blips represented the Doctor's men, rough and ready soldiers he had handpicked from faraway places like Austria, the Czech Republic, and Poland. Two fluorescent blue blips symbolized the kids—Axel Jack and Daisha Tandala.

And at this moment, the Doctor hated them both.

"What's the weather report on the East Coast today?" the Doctor asked.

Pinchole punched a key on his computer. "Our meteorologist reports nothing but sun and blue skies for the next three days from Ohio to New England. That means lots of solar energy for the tracking devices."

The Doctor glanced at Pinchole and let out an audible grunt. The fact that his men's GeoPort trackers only worked with solar energy irked him to no end. Pinchole and his Satellite Warp technicians had been working for months to figure out why the trackers' batteries completely drained when the Pursuers followed Daisha and Axel through the Warp. All of their attempts at a fix had met with failure.

The Satellite Warp—or just the Warp, as they called it—was the Doctor's grandest achievement. The program had begun as an experiment to detect gravitational waves in the fabric of space-time as predicted by Albert Einstein. Hardly anyone—chiefly the Doctor himself and the former research scientists he had funded, Stanford professors Roswell Jack and Jodiann

Tandala—knew that Einstein's theory of a rotating mass distorting the space and time around it could also transport a human being to any location on the planet. Simply by harnessing the power of the solar wind and using GPS coordinates.

Precisely, one needed GPS coordinates and a handheld geographical transportation system—GeoPort for short. Professors Jack and Tandala had made only two, both of which were now in the hands of their rogue children.

Pinchole pointed to the monitor. "It looks like the boy and girl are slipping away."

Both watched as the two blue blips distanced themselves from the four red blips. Soon the blue blips disappeared altogether, and the red blips fell hopelessly behind.

The Doctor tossed his hands up in disgust. "This was our chance!" he roared. "The girl's GeoPort plopped her into a desolate cornfield, for crying out loud!"

"The day isn't over yet," Pinchole said, glancing at his watch. "Night won't fall for another eight hours and thirteen minutes. The Pursuers can easily pick up their trail."

"That is so reassuring," the Doctor said sarcastically. "It will be just like when the Pursuers picked up their trail in Brazil, South Africa, New Zealand, Liechtenstein, and a half dozen other places. How can two thirteen-year-old kids be so hard to hunt down?"

"You've often said it yourself, Doctor. The boy and girl have their parents' brains and..."

The Doctor slapped his flat palm on the desktop. "That's enough from you! Just get those trackers to work on batteries so we can hunt them at night. If those kids find this Magnes Solace before me, heads will roll."

"Yes, sir," Pinchole said and walked out of the Monitoring Room. The Doctor instructed a new SWT—Satellite Warp technician—to expand the topographical view. The farther the kids moved away from the Pursuers, the worse the contrast on the monitors became.

As the Doctor was about to scold the SWT for expanding the view too fast, a burning sensation flashed across the left side of his face. He reached up and felt his cheek. His skin was hot, almost scorching to the touch.

The Doctor immediately left the Monitoring Room and burst into the nearest bathroom. His heart raced in his chest, his hands shook, and the left side of his face flamed even hotter. He turned on the faucet, filled his cupped hands with cold water, and splashed his face. The sensation gave him a glorious but temporary reprieve. After a moment, the heat and uncomfortable burning sensation returned in full fury. The Doctor took a deep breath and looked into the mirror. No matter how many appointments with dermatologists and therapists, the simple act of looking at his reflection in a bathroom mirror almost always sent him spiraling into a panic attack.

Nevus flammeus, the scientific name for the large port-wine stain covering the left side of his face since birth, stared back at him.

"Doctor Stain," he whispered to himself. "Those idiots think I don't know what they call me behind my back."

The Doctor ran his finger around the edges of the stain, tracing the elongated peanut shape that he had since childhood. All of his Silicon Valley billions and twenty-two-thousand-square-foot mansion couldn't take the shame away. The bright-red birthmark was both his god and devil, fueling his drive to succeed and humiliating him at the same time. He would not allow Axel and Daisha to destroy his plans. The chase for the GeoPorts was not a high-tech game of hide-and-seek, but a war for control of everything—money, culture, politics, and power.

The Doctor's skin was slowly returning to a normal temperature, but the anger in his heart was still raging.

He dried his dripping face with a towel and went back to the Monitoring Room. The dash to catch the kids and get back the GeoPorts was a game he did not want to miss.

Chapter Four

AXEL

Axel dropped his hot dog on the sidewalk and took off down the street.

"Get him!" he heard one of the Pursuers shout, only the accent made it sound more like "*Geet heem*!"

"The endless sprint," Axel huffed to himself as he ran. His life for the past six months had been one endless race—Daisha and him against the Pursuers. The Doctor's men would never stop chasing them, and he and Daisha would never stop running from them.

All because of the earth-shattering scientific breakthrough his dad and Daisha's mom had stumbled upon in a messy lab tucked into the basement of Stanford University's Varian Physics Building.

"Watch where you're going, jerk!" a portly man wearing a gray suit barked as Axel came within millimeters of plowing into him.

"Sorry," Axel mumbled and took a quick glance over his shoulder.

The Pursuers were less than twenty yards away, charging in his direction. He ran faster, his backpack bouncing up and down on his shoulders. The pack slowed him down, but he couldn't drop it. Everything he owned was inside—changes of clothes, extra shoes, US passport, and a 10 GB flash drive filled with family photos.

"Stop him!" one of the Pursuers shouted at passersby. "He stole from me! Thief!"

Throngs of people stopped in the middle of the sidewalk, gawking at the sudden commotion. Axel ran past them and saw a tall woman with short blond hair hurry down a set of stairs leading to the subway. He followed right behind her. A rush of dank, stale-smelling air hit him in the face as he ran down a long corridor. Loud footsteps coming from behind him meant the Pursuers were close.

Gates and turnstiles blocked the end of the underground hallway. Axel saw a row of ATM-looking machines selling something called a MetroCard. Commuters swiped the card and passed through the turnstiles. Axel didn't have time to buy a card and follow the rules. Without a moment of hesitation, he leaped over the turnstile and ran down the dimly lit platform.

Dozens of people were standing behind a wide yellow line. Some played with their phones or stared at reading devices; others glanced impatiently down the dark train tunnel, waiting for their next connection. Axel looked too. He saw a distant set of headlights rumbling down the tracks.

A woman's loud gasp made him look up. He saw that one of the Pursuers had knocked over an old lady as he was clumsily climbing over the turnstiles without paying. A crowd of concerned citizens rushed to help her. Three young men came at the Pursuers, yelling at them to apologize. The tall Pursuer closed his fists and punched two of the men square in the face. The shorter, heavier Pursuer yanked a handgun from his jacket pocket and pistol-whipped the other one.

Frightened screams echoed down the platform at the sight of a gun. People ducked for cover. Parents clutched children close; others dialed cell phones, presumably calling 911. Axel hid behind a large steel support beam at the end of the platform. His pulse raced as the subway train's headlights grew closer, but they were still far from the station.

"Has anyone seen a boy with long, curly brown

hair wearing a backpack?" one of the Pursuers asked the crowd.

"We know he's here somewhere," said the other.

Axel peeked around the support beam and saw a trembling bald man with thick glasses point in his direction.

"That's the kid you want," the bald guy said. "He's at the end of the platform."

As the Pursuers ran toward him, the train tore into the stop. A loud *ding-dong* sounded, the train doors opened wide, and crowds of unsuspecting people poured out.

A computerized-sounding female voice rang out from an intercom, "This is Twenty-Third Street. Transfer available to..."

Axel didn't hear what she said next. He took advantage of the bustle and jumped into the subway car. The Pursuers pushed past the crowd and ran toward Axel, wicked smiles plastered across their faces. As they closed in on him, another computerized voice blurted out, "Watch the closing doors, please."

There was another *ding-dong* sound. The subway doors began to shut, but not before the shorter Pursuer managed to stick his pistol-laden hand between the closing doors. The train lurched forward, sending Axel tumbling to the floor.

The train slowly rolled out of the station with the Pursuer's hand still stuck between the doors. A look of panic washed across the Pursuer's face. He ran alongside the train, desperately trying to yank his hand free. His gun fired wildly in Axel's direction. The bullets shattered windows and pierced holes in the seats. They came so close to hitting Axel that he could hear the bullets fly by his ear.

Finally the Pursuer wriggled his hand free from the subway doors and fell back onto the platform. The train whizzed out the station and into the dark depths of the tunnel.

Chapter Five

DAISHA

Daisha had more in common with an antelope than just her running ability. Her last name—Tandala—was the Swahili word for *antelope* in her deceased father's native Kenya. She needed every bit of her namesake's strength to outdistance the Pursuers who were closing in fast.

"Don't make me shoot!" one of the Pursuers shouted.

The cornfield gave way to a pitted dirt road snaked with tractor wheel tracks. She bounded across the road, heading for the woods and the path the boy had told her about. A gunshot blasted over her head. The bullet struck a low-hanging tree branch and sprayed wood chips into her eyes, temporarily blinding her. Daisha stumbled into the weeds and crumpled to the ground.

"You hit her!" she heard one of the Pursuers say. "Doctor Stain wanted her alive if possible."

"Well, in this case," said the other, "it was not possible."

Daisha gently wiped the back of her hand across her eyes. Her vision was blurry, but she could see the well-worn path described by the boy. She jumped to her feet and started running again. The Pursuers had gained on her because of the fall. They were now less than fifteen yards behind.

"Stop!" a Pursuer barked. "Or I'll shoot again!"

Although the boy had described the natural bridge over the creek as a fallen tree, it was really more like a large, lightning-struck limb. Daisha placed her right foot on the bridge, which was no wider than her sneaker. She clutched her satchel and placed her left foot on the limb. The Pursuers were racing toward her with guns drawn.

"Right foot, left foot, right foot, left..." she chanted, tightroping her way across the bridge to the creek bank on the other side.

The Pursuers fired a round of bullets at her from the opposite side of the creek, but all missed their mark. Daisha ducked behind a tree, gasping for breath. She watched as the two Pursuers attempted to scurry over the bridge. The first one took four tentative steps before tumbling into the muddy water. The other one made it slightly farther, but he, too, quickly lost his balance. A round of loud cursing from the Pursuers echoed through the woods.

"I hope the leeches suck out every last drop of your blood!" Daisha shouted at them.

"We're going to suck your blood!" a Pursuer hollered back.

Daisha picked up a rock, hurled it at them, and then raced down the path. The woods soon gave way to an expansive grassy lawn. A large sign read *Welcome to the Mount Vernon Water Park.* She saw a huge yellow waterslide, two Olympic-sized pools, and a spray park for little kids. Swimmers packed the place. Shouts and squeals reverberated around the pool. Kids and adults screamed happily as they slid down the waterslide and splashed into the deep water. She scanned the crowd carefully, hoping someone she didn't know would walk over to her and say, "You must be Daisha. I'm Magnes Solace, and I believe you have something for me."

But Daisha had no time for such fantasies. She turned and saw the two sopping-wet Pursuers emerge from the woods. They saw her standing next to the fence surrounding the pool and continued the chase.

"This is my horrible life," she said to herself after quickly tightening her shoelaces. "Run, hide, run, hide, get shot at, and run some more."

The GeoPort in her front pocket buzzed as the Pursuers zeroed in on her location with the tracking device. She took a deep breath and started running again, this time a loping jog to try to conserve energy. Tears welled in her eyes as she moved across a busy road and into a residential area of small houses. She wasn't crying for herself, but for her mother, Axel's father, and even Axel.

Axel was the only one on the entire planet who could make her feel better, but he was who-knew-where and she was here. The Warp took twenty-four hours to reset. That meant she would have to flee from the Pursuers for a whole day before she could punch another set of coordinates into the GeoPort and get out of Ohio.

The cat-and-mouse game with the Pursuers lasted for the rest of the day and into the early evening. The chase took her through neighborhoods, school athletic fields, and dinky downtown Mount Vernon, and into the outskirts of town with acres of cornfields. Only when the sun went down did Daisha feel safe. The solar trackers were useless in the dark, but to give herself distance from the Pursuers for the next morning's inevitable chase, Daisha continued to walk until the moon was high in the sky.

"It's got to be midnight," Daisha said, then plopped down at the base of a large tree. Every fiber of muscle in her body ached with exhaustion. She fumbled around in her satchel and found a bottle of water and a half-eaten chocolate Clif Bar. As she ate, her thoughts drifted back to life before GeoPorts, Satellite Warps, and the Doctor. A smile came to her face as she remembered the family bungalow in the University South section of Palo Alto. Her mother and Axel's father were colleagues and best friends. One of Daisha's earliest memories was of playing with Axel at Centennial Fountain in front of the Green Library. The space was a whispering gallery, which meant the two of them could stand on different sides of the fountain and hear each other's every word even though they were far apart.

"I wish we could do that now, Axel," Daisha whispered softly to herself. The coordinates she had committed to memory flashed in her mind.

37.4302° N, 122.1288° W

Her eyelids grew heavy, and she drifted off to sleep.

Chapter Six

AXEL

The last words his father and Daisha's mother ever spoke echoed in Axel's mind.

The Doctor wants to use them for very bad things, but you two can't let him. Take them to Magnes Solace! his father had cried.

Only the electron diffusion region can destroy them, Daisha's mother whispered. *The coordinates are Latitude 23.1483...*

Before Daisha's mother could finish the coordinates, gunfire tore through the trees. Axel and Daisha had watched in horror as bullets mortally wounded their parents. They'd looked up and seen six men rushing toward them. One of the men aimed his gun directly at them.

"Let's get out of here!" Daisha had screamed. "They're going to shoot us too!"

With a push of a button, Axel and Daisha were gone. There was nothing left of them but a puff of white smoke and a blast of electrical discharge.

* * *

The jostle of the train knocked Axel back to the present. He sat up straight and rubbed his tired eyes. The *Doctor* his father had referred to was Doctor Lennon Hatch, the zillionaire who'd funded their parents' work. He and Daisha also knew that what the Doctor craved so desperately was now in their hands. This was why the man had killed their parents and wouldn't stop until they were dead too. But Axel had made a promise to his father that day. He was going to figure out where to find this Magnes Solace person and destroy the GeoPorts.

But the mystery of Magnes Solace was a puzzle Axel and Daisha had yet to solve.

"Twenty-four hours," Axel muttered as the subway train sped down the tracks.

He glanced down at his GeoPort. Actually, the time was down to only twenty-one hours and forty-seven minutes before the Warp reset and he could punch in the coordinates to get out of New York City.

But where would he go?

He and Daisha had made an emergency contingency plan in case of separation. They would meet back at the

Hoover Park Dog Run, where their journey had begun. He had memorized the coordinates by heart.

37.4302° N, 122.1288° W

Home.

And when the two hooked up again, they'd walk to their favorite restaurant, Ammar's Hummus Shop. Axel would order a side of falafel and a big plate of chicken skewers and wash it all down with a glass of cold lemonade.

His stomach growled just thinking of food. He'd spent the last of his money on the hot dog and didn't even have a chance to enjoy a single bite.

"One Hundred and Twenty-Fifth Street," a male voice announced from the subway intercom. "Watch the closing doors."

Hordes of people came and went as the train wound its way around the city. Axel rode the rails for the next few hours, hopping on a different train every couple stops, avoiding the Pursuers. As he rode, he cupped the GeoPort between his hands, feeling its warm and steady rhythmic hum. The little device was like holding a cyborg's beating heart. His father and Daisha's mother had invented the world's most advanced technological organ. But instead of pumping synthetic blood to give physiological life to a mechanical person, this heart transported a real human being to any place on Earth with the press of a button.

The GeoPort's concept was actually very simple. But learning how to manipulate the device was a lot of trial and error. The device worked like those simple handheld GPS units he had used in Boy Scouts for geocaching. But when he and Daisha punched in latitude and longitude coordinates, instead of just *showing* them how to get to a location, the GeoPort plopped them there in a matter of seconds.

Unfortunately, sometimes those latitude and longitude coordinates included bodies of water. One of the first times he and Daisha had used the GeoPorts, they'd learned that wet lesson the hard way. They had carelessly typed out a set of random coordinates without first investigating their destination. The Warp transported them from the frenetic French Quarter in New Orleans directly into a crocodile-infested swamp deep in the Australian bush. The two of them had spent hours clinging to tree branches just out of reach of several hungry, man-eating reptiles. Thankfully, a local crab fisherman eventually boated past and rescued them.

Insights about the GeoPort came fast and furious after that. They learned that the devices needed twenty-four hours to reset and had highly sophisticated DNA security encoding. The GeoPorts operated only with their specific DNA. When they touched the devices, a sensor scanned their skin cells. Wearing gloves was a big no-no when trying to turn on the GeoPort.

The worst thing about the GeoPorts was how they had come to possess Axel and Daisha. After their parents' frantic call to meet at the Hoover Park Dog Run, he and Daisha had only minutes to glean information on how to use the GeoPorts before the Doctor's Pursuers shot their parents in cold blood.

Don't run from who you are.

Aslan's advice to Lucy in *The Voyage of the Dawn Treader* popped into Axel's brain. He loved all the Narnia books and could recite whole passages from memory because he had read them so many times. He used to fantasize that flying through the Warp was like the Pevensie siblings stepping into the wardrobe and entering another world. After months of running from the Doctor, the comparison now felt shallow. Narnia was an imaginary world of made-up characters and places. The Warp was real. His personal White Witch was the Red-Faced Man. The Pursuers were his wolves, Black Dwarves, and Giants all rolled into one.

Chapter Seven
DAISHA

As Daisha drifted deeper into sleep, images of the first time she had laid eyes on the Doctor a year before flooded her dreams. Her mother had been planning the dinner for a week. She was making her specialty: Jamaican jerk chicken served with coconut rice and peas and for dessert a scrumptious Caribbean black fruitcake.

"I hope the cake is low sugar," Daisha said, placing silverware on the dining room table. "The nurse at school said too much sugar is bad for you."

Her mother rolled her eyes. "A little sugar once in a while isn't going to hurt anybody. How often do I make my fruitcake?"

"Only for special occasions, like my birthday, Christmas, Thanksgiving."

"And when I'm trying to impress my extremely

wealthy research sponsor," her mother interrupted. "Now, my dear *solis*, go put on that *decorus vestio* your *avia* sent from Port Royal."

"Speak English please!" Daisha protested.

Her mother laughed. "Go put on the *beautiful dress* your *grandmother* sent you. I'll have you speaking and understanding Latin before you're a teenager, heaven help me."

Daisha rolled her eyes and went into her room to change. Her mother was always spouting about how the study of Latin trained the mind and made speaking different languages much easier. Daisha was starting to pick up on many of the words, but she refused to let her mother know.

The dress was what her grandmother back in Jamaica called a traditional *quadrille dress*. Her mother simply called it a *bandanna dress*, and Daisha liked that name much better. The skirt was red, white, and maroon, and the dress came with ruffled sleeves. It was beautiful, but she refused to wear the head tie. She changed out of her T-shirt and shorts into the new outfit.

"Ta-da!" Daisha announced, bursting from her room. She swished cheekily around the couch, nearly knocking over a table lamp.

"Beautiful," her mother said. "You look like a—"

The doorbell rang.

"Is it him?" Daisha asked.

Her mother nodded and pulled her daughter into the kitchen. "I need to tell you something before I open the door," she said. "His name is Doctor Lennon Hatch. Only he's not a real doctor."

"Then why does he call himself one?"

"Vanity, I guess. A university in Arizona gave him an honorary doctorate because he donated the money for a new building, but that's not important. He has a very large birthmark on the side of his face that can be alarming at first."

The doorbell rang again.

"Do not stare," her mother instructed.

Daisha nodded. Her mother ran to answer the door. Daisha had no idea what her mother had meant by a birthmark, but when the Doctor stepped from the foyer into the living room, she understood immediately. The whole left side of man's face was extremely red.

The Doctor smiled wide at Daisha and reached for her hand. "You must be Daisha," he said.

Daisha giggled uncomfortably and pulled her hand away. His palm was cold and sweaty, and she did not like the look in his eyes.

"I brought this for you," the Doctor said, handing her

mother a bottle of wine.

"You shouldn't have," her mother said.

"It's a bottle of 1986 Château Mouton Rothschild, and it only set me back a thousand dollars."

Her mother's mouth dropped open. "I...uh...um..." she stuttered. "I don't know whether to drink this or put it in my safety deposit box at the bank."

The Doctor laughed. "Wine is for drinking. Money is for the bank and for funding your amazing work."

Her mother smiled at the Doctor and led him into the living room. They took a seat while the Doctor popped the cork and poured two glasses of wine. Daisha excused herself to the kitchen and chugged a glass of lemonade. The man freaked her out, and she wanted to get away from him as quickly as possible. But that didn't stop her from eavesdropping on them.

"I wish Roswell could be here tonight," her mother said.

"No need for him right now," the Doctor said. "I wanted to spend the evening with just you and your precious daughter."

"She's a bit shy. I hope you understand."

"Most children are in my presence. Now, tell me more about your groundbreaking work. I have to say that I was quite stunned when you told me about your breakthrough."

Her mother stood up from her chair and took a seat next to the Doctor on the couch. "The technology is going to change the world," she said.

"And make me an even wealthier and more powerful man," the Doctor added.

"The Satellite Warp and geographical transportation aren't just about money—they're about making the world a better place."

Daisha peeked around the corner and listened intently. She had only been vaguely aware of her mother's work but wanted to know more.

"The first tests have been phenomenally successful," her mother explained. "Both Roswell and I are convinced that within a year the Warp will be up and running."

"And its New York Stock Exchange ticker symbol up and running as well?"

"Is money all you think about?"

"No. I think about you a lot too."

Her mother flashed him an uncomfortable look and scooted slightly farther down on the couch.

"Just imagine all the good things that will happen, thanks to the Warp," she continued. "If you were in San Francisco and needed to be in Miami, you could just set the GeoPort's coordinates and be there in seconds. Say good-bye to pollution, traffic, and ugly freeways.

Instantly, you could have food for starving children in any part of the world, no need for ships, airplanes, trains, cars, or motorcycles. Greenhouse gases could be history, stinky combustion engines as outdated as a horse and carriage. We'll be heroes of the environment. They'll name high schools and airports after..."

Daisha watched in horror as the Doctor lunged at her mother. He wrapped his arms around her shoulders and planted a wet, sloppy, and unwelcomed kiss on her lips.

"Stop!" her mother blurted out. "This isn't what I invited you here for."

"Mom!" Daisha shouted from the kitchen, trying to diffuse the situation. "The chicken's done!"

"Thank you, Daisha," her mother answered. "I'll be right there."

Daisha stepped into the living room as her mother rushed toward the kitchen. The Doctor was staring at her, an angry look on his flaming face.

"Do you want to be a scientist like your mother?" he asked.

"I think so," Daisha answered.

"Then you'll need very wealthy investors like me to fund your work. Did you know that?"

Daisha shook her head.

The Doctor stood up and walked over to her. "Use this experience as a lesson, young lady. If you take up the science trade, always treat your sponsors with respect or the money may dry up."

"Dinner's ready," her mother said, stepping back into the living room.

The Doctor grabbed his jacket and walked to the front door. "Please, accept my apologies," he said. "I have been called away on urgent business. Keep the bottle of wine, and don't worry about your funding. I wouldn't stop supporting you for anything in the world."

The front door slammed, and the Doctor was gone. Tears gushed from her mother's eyes, and she ran into her bedroom. Daisha just stood there, shocked at what had happened in her own house.

A year later, the Warp was up and running. Her mother and Axel's father were dead, and she and Axel were running for their lives.

Chapter Eight
DOCTOR STAIN

As darkness descended over Ohio and New York City, stillness fell over the Monitoring Room on the third floor of the Doctor's headquarters in the heart of Silicon Valley. The modest sign in front of the building read: Hatch Management, LLC. To the outside world, the Doctor was a highly successful, multibillionaire hedge-fund manager with a love for science. The inside of his building told a much different story.

The first floor was typical office cubicles, conference rooms, an employee break area, and a well-stocked supply closet. The next five floors were part of the most sophisticated satellite control center in the world. More than a hundred scientists—each sworn to secrecy—manned wall-to-wall computers, antenna systems, communications modulators, signal conversion systems, subcarrier synthesizers, and dozens of other pieces of high-tech equipment. The Doctor dedicated the top floor to his conventional reconnaissance satellite and to the Jack-Tandala satellite (named after the inventors) that harnessed the sun's solar wind and made geographical transportation possible.

"Tomorrow's sunrise in New York City is 5:33 a.m.," Pinchole said. "Central Ohio's rise-and-shine is 6:08 a.m. The Pursuers' trackers should take exactly nine minutes to recharge and be up and running."

"And the chase begins again," the Doctor said with a sigh.

"They can't run forever. Their time will run out soon."

"Power everything down, and meet me in my office. We need to talk." The Doctor grabbed his personal laptop and left the room.

Without sunlight, the trackers could not work; without detectable trackers, the reconnaissance satellite could not follow the action on the ground. Pinchole instructed his SWTs to place the computers on sleep mode. The constant whine of the equipment's cooling fans fell silent, making the Monitoring Room eerily quiet. Weary-eyed SWTs collected their belongings, double-checked the locks and passwords, and followed Pinchole down the hallway. They would all be back early at 4:15 a.m. for another day of high-tech hide-and-seek.

The Doctor had a spacious office suite with a view of Googleplex, the corporate headquarters of Google, Inc. He still remembered the day two scruffy Stanford students named Larry Page and Sergey Brin had approached him about investing in their Internet search engine company. The kids had impressed him, so he wrote them a check for two hundred thousand dollars on the spot. The simple investment had made him millions.

A knock came at his office door.

"Come in," he said.

Pinchole stepped inside, took off his lab coat, and sat down on a leather couch. Dark circles rimmed his bloodshot eyes. "I'm starving," he said.

"I've ordered us dinner from Maki," the Doctor said. "I hope you like sushi."

Pinchole nodded his approval. "The solar wind gives, and the solar wind takes away."

"What do you mean?" the Doctor asked.

"Thanks to Einstein's theory of a space and time bend, Professors Jack and Tandala figured out how to use space magnets to capture the electrons found in the solar wind. Once technicians transfer the electrons to Earth via infrared lasers, the massive amount of energy gives us the ability to dematerialize the elemental composition of the human body to a stream of charged particles. We then use the GeoPort to reconstitute those particles back to human form and transfer them to any latitudinal and longitudinal point on Earth."

"*We* don't do anything," the Doctor said with disgust. "It's those two kids who are doing all the reconstituting and transferring."

"We need to locate the mysterious Magnes Solace. Several of our men stated that before the professors... ahem...left the project, they were overheard instructing their kids to take the GeoPorts to this person."

The Doctor twisted the cap on a bottle of water and took a huge gulp. "Then we have to find those kids before they find Magnes Solace."

"We are working very hard on that. For some yet-unknown reason, the charged particles released from the solar wind drain the batteries in the tracking units as they go through the Warp. Solar energy works just fine, though."

"Solace is an odd name. Are you sure the men heard it correctly?"

"Again, that's what every man in the dog park said. I have some of my best Googlers scouring the Internet for any reference to Magnes Solace. The most interesting thing they've come up with so far is a fourteenth-century reference to a man named Robert Solace from the *Calendar of Letter-Books of the City of London*."

"I don't need an Ancestry.com lesson. I want to know who this person is and why Axel and Daisha were instructed to find him...or her."

"Magnes Solace obviously must have been working with the professors on the GeoPort. If we find this person before the kids, we can sit back and wait for them to arrive."

A voice rang out through the intercom.

"Doctor," a woman's voice said. "Your dinner is here."

"Thank you," the Doctor said. "Please bring it to my office."

A young woman with shoulder-length platinum-blond hair came into the room and laid out their food on a table. "Will you need anything else tonight, sir?" she asked.

"That will be all, Kari. Have a pleasant evening, and I'll see you tomorrow."

Pinchole tore into the miso soup and shrimp tempura appetizers like a ravenous dog. "You know, the Warp is infinite just like space. But you need a GeoPort or tracker to get into it. I wish we could have gleaned more information from the professors before they..."

"They had to go," the Doctor said abruptly. "You are

the main science man now. I don't want their names mentioned around me again. And change the official name of the Jack-Tandala satellite to the Doctor Lennon Hatch satellite."

"The two of them were such brilliant physicists. They knew the ins and outs of this thing better than any man alive did. The Warp was their baby."

The Doctor took a sip of green tea and nibbled on a California roll. "This is your baby now, Pinchole," he said. "And it's time for you to take off the diapers and learn to potty by yourself."

"It's still unbelievable how those two kids stole the only working GeoPorts in the world. We don't even know how to make another one," Pinchole said, digging into the sashimi rolls. "Fortunately, we have the technology on how to track the darn things."

"Those *darn things* are the greatest technological advancement of mankind," the Doctor reminded him. "The Warp and GeoPorts are more powerful and will be more profitable than a million nuclear power plants."

Pinchole sat up to grab a bottle of water when his cell phone rang. "It's Stetson," he said. "He's one of my top SWTs." He punched in the phone's pass code and hit the speaker button. "Hello?"

"Mr. Pinchole," Stetson's nervous voice echoed from

the speaker.

"Yes," Pinchole said. "I'm with the Doctor, and you're on speaker."

"You need to come down to the Monitoring Room. My team and I have something to show you."

"We're in the middle of dinner. Can this wait?"

"No. It can't wait."

"What is it?" the Doctor asked, raising his voice.

"It's the GeoPort tracking devices. We've figured out what's causing the batteries to drain while transporting through the Warp. We've corrected the problem remotely. As of five minutes ago, the Pursuers are able to track the GeoPorts at night."

The Doctor and Pinchole looked at each other with the same excited expressions. They dropped their chopsticks and rushed as fast as they could to the Monitoring Room.

Chapter Nine

AXEL

Axel quickly figured out that the New York City subway system was a great way to dodge the Pursuers. The underground trains were even better than the busy streets of Ho Chi Minh City. Without direct sun, the solar trackers were only able to store enough power for an hour or so. That meant the Pursuers could only hunt him for a short time before having to leave the subway system and recharge their trackers.

He carefully studied a subway map. His journey had begun at the Twenty-Third Street Station on a Q train. He then rode north through Manhattan and into Queens to where the tracks ended at a place called Astoria-Ditmars Boulevard. After backtracking and changing to the D train, he was at Coney Island and Stillwell Avenue.

The train was now traveling above ground, and

he watched the sun disappear over the horizon. He glanced at his watch. The time was eight thirty-six in the evening. Darkness fell over the city. The Pursuers' trackers temporarily could not locate him.

Axel wandered out of the train station and into the busy streets. Hundreds of people strolled up and down the sidewalks. The place was all lit up. Live music blared from an elevated stage. A huge Ferris wheel slowly spun in the distance. The smell of hot dogs, cotton candy, pizza, and other luscious food smells filled his nostrils.

"I'm so hungry I could eat a dead rat," Axel said to himself as he blended into the crowd.

As he walked closer to the beach, he saw a huge outdoor movie screen playing an action-adventure film. He heard the whining engines of go-carts as they whizzed around a track. Little kids rushed to and from all the different amusements and carnival games, their cheeks smeared with sticky cotton candy. Parents, couples, old people, and gangs of teenagers strolled up and down the boardwalk. The place looked like so much fun, and he wished Daisha could be here with him.

"Yuck!" A girl's disgusted voice yelled out from behind him. "I forgot how much I hate corn dogs!"

Axel turned and saw a girl with large hoop earrings

and wearing cut-off shorts set down on the rail of the boardwalk a fresh corn dog with a bite taken out of it. His mouth began to water, his stomach grumbled in hunger, and without so much as a second thought, Axel plucked the corn dog off the rail and ran down to the beach.

Ocean waves gently rolled on the sand. The New York City skyline burned brilliantly in the distance. Axel pinched off the girl's bite mark with his fingertips, and shoved the entire corn dog into his mouth. The golden batter was still warm, the encased hot dog juicy and succulent. The only thing that could have made his dinner any better was a dollop of ketchup for dipping.

With his stomach temporarily satisfied, he walked along the beach. Hermit crabs scuttled across the sand. Many people were still splashing around, but the beach wasn't nearly as crowded as the boardwalk. When he came to a large pier jutting into the ocean, he took a quick look over his shoulder to see if anyone was looking and then dashed to a dry spot beneath.

He rested in the sand, completely oblivious to the raucous party noise going on all around him. One day without Daisha was too long, and he had made his decision. He would ride the New York City subways until tomorrow, trying his best to outsmart the Pursuers who would surely be back on his trail come morning. At noon when the Warp reset, he'd punch in the coordinates to their prearranged spot at the dog park in Palo Alto. He hoped that his friend would make the same decision.

Her husky voice echoed in his head. "Let's just get rid of these stupid things," she'd always say. "We'll never find Magnes Solace."

If he had a dollar for every time Daisha talked about throwing away the GeoPorts, he'd have enough money for a large pepperoni pizza and an order of fried mozzarella sticks right now. He too often fantasized about chucking his GeoPort into the garbage. But getting rid of their parents' work would not be so easy.

"Besides," Axel mused. "They said to take the GeoPorts to Magnes Solace. The GeoPorts can only be destroyed in one of the electron diffusion regions, wherever and whatever the heck that is."

Who was this Magnes Solace person anyway? The identity was a complete mystery to him. He didn't even know if Magnes was a boy or girl. Daisha and he had spent hours in a Vietnamese Internet café googling the name. There was nothing, not one online mention of the person. The only hope they had of finding him or her was to figure out the rest of the coordinate numbers

Daisha's mother had managed to spit out before a bullet pierced her heart.

Latitude 23.1483...

He knew the latitude number specified the north-south position of a point on Earth's surface. But the partial coordinates were not enough to find anything. He needed both the latitude and longitude coordinates to have any hope of finding Magnes Solace.

A teenage couple ran under the pier, interrupting his thoughts. Axel pushed himself deeper into the sand. He watched as they sucked face for a good five minutes and then ran off hand in hand.

When the lovebirds disappeared, he let his thoughts drift back to Warping home. Materializing in the middle of Palo Alto was risky—maybe even suicidal—but the running had to stop. He wondered how his friends back home were spending their summer. Probably getting ready for high school, surfing at Half Moon Bay, skating at Greer Park, taking the bus to Great America amusement park in Santa Clara, and a hundred other fun things.

Axel's eyes fought to stay open. His head bobbed like a fishing buoy as he tried to stay awake. The sound of soft footsteps in the sand filled his ears. For a dozing moment, he wasn't sure if they were real or just the echoes of a dream. The sound grew louder, and his eyes snapped open. He saw what looked like two bright, bloody eyeballs slicing through the darkness. They were actually two men carrying flashlights, walking calmly toward him. His GeoPort throbbed to life. When the men were within ten yards of his bed in the sand, he knew exactly who they were.

The Pursuers had followed his trail directly to the beach.

Chapter Ten
DOCTOR STAIN

An excited roar came from Pinchole and the other SWTs inside the Monitoring Room.

The Doctor, who had been outside in the hallway, flung open the door. "What's going on in here?" he asked.

Pinchole was pumping his fists in the air like he had just scored the winning touchdown in the Super Bowl. "They got him!"

"Got whom?" the Doctor asked.

"The boy!" Pinchole exclaimed. "The Pursuers captured Axel Jack!"

The Doctor eyed Pinchole suspiciously. "You had better not be pulling my leg."

"Absolutely not, sir. Look at the monitor."

The Doctor stared intently at the large screen. Usually when he scanned the view, Axel and Daisha were distancing themselves from the Pursuers. Blue blips represented the kids; red blips represented his Pursuers. Now, there was no blue or red, but one large magenta-colored pulsing dot.

"What does this mean?" the Doctor asked.

"Red and blue mixed together make magenta," Pinchole explained. "That means one of our men and the boy are on top of each other. Understand?"

"No, I don't understand. I want more proof than an elementary-school art lesson."

A loud buzzing sound came from a speaker on the satellite console.

"A transmission is coming through," announced one of the SWT assistants.

"Quiet, everyone," the Doctor ordered.

Silence fell over the Monitoring Room. The only sounds were the equipment's cooling fans and the crackle of radio static.

"We have...captured...boy," a man's voice with a thick European accent said. "GeoPort...in our...possession. Return with prisoner...when Warp...resets...over."

An audible gasp escaped the Doctor's lips. His pulse raced, and the hair on his arms stood on end. He quickly scanned his memory, making sure he had taken his blood pressure medication that morning.

"What about the girl?" the Doctor asked.

"Of course," Pinchole said, changing the view on the screen. "I was so excited about the boy's capture that I had momentarily forgotten about her."

The map quickly faded from New York City to central Ohio. To Pinchole's astonishment, he did not see red or blue blips, but one large magenta dot just like with Axel.

"Look!" Pinchole exclaimed. "They must have the girl too!"

Another cheer went up from the SWTs, and in a rare moment of unrestrained emotion, the Doctor reached out and patted Pinchole on the back.

"Are you absolutely sure our men have her?" the Doctor asked.

"We haven't heard a transmission from them yet," Pinchole said. "But the meshing of the two colors into magenta is a direct hit. You saw it for yourself with the capture of the boy. Unless..."

Pinchole's voice trailed off, making the Doctor inquire deeper.

"Unless what?" the Doctor asked, narrowing his eyebrows.

"Our surveillance satellites are not actually tracking the people. They are following and gathering information from chips that professors Jack and Tandala placed inside the solar tracker and the GeoPort. So, unless the girl has somehow gotten hold of the solar tracker and—"

"And that is highly unlikely," the Doctor said, cutting him off.

"Exactly. I have a better chance of sprouting fairy wings and flying to Ohio than that girl has of overpowering two of our men and stealing the tracker."

"Then let's wait for their transmission. In the meantime, we have a lot to talk about."

Pinchole ran a hand through his thinning mousy-brown hair and let out a deep sigh. "Now the real fun begins."

"I want to review the plans down to the very last detail," the Doctor said. "Follow me to my office."

Once inside the Doctor's spacious, opulent office, Pinchole went over the strategy he had been fine-tuning for over a year. First, they were to secure the kids, make them comfortable, and then pick their brains about practical use of the GeoPort. After all, they had been the ones using the devices and were the experts. While all this was going on, Pinchole and his SWTs would carefully break down the parts of the GeoPort to begin mass production. The Doctor would hole up with a small army of lawyers and lobbyists—registering patents, wining and dining the heads of the US Federal Transit Administration and Security and Exchange Commission, bigwigs from the National Aeronautics and Space Administration, even the president of the United States and other world leaders.

After all the t's were crossed and the i's dotted, the Doctor Lennon Hatch Geographical Transportation Company would be up and running, and he would be the most celebrated and powerful man on Earth.

"Can you believe this is about to become a reality?" Pinchole mused.

"I won't break open a bottle of Château Margaux until the first wealthy business traveler pays a small fortune to use the GeoPort for instant transport from Wall Street to the Tokyo Stock Exchange," the Doctor said.

"What do we do with the kids once we have gleaned all the information we can from them?" Pinchole asked.

The Doctor stared at the sprawling Googleplex headquarters out his window. A superior smirk washed over his face. The Google founders had made themselves billionaires and many of their stockholders millionaires with a simple search engine company. They gave people the ability to look up information instantaneously. He would give the people the ability to travel anywhere instantaneously. The Doctor would be king, and everyone else in Silicon Valley his court jesters.

"The boy we'll have no use for," the Doctor answered finally. "I haven't decided what to do with the girl."

"Well, I'd very much like to hear a transmission signaling that our men have in fact captured her."

"They have her," the Doctor said confidently. "You said it yourself—red and blue make magenta. The GeoPort and I make history."

"With the GeoPorts soon to be in our possession, we don't have to find the mysterious Magnes Solace anymore," Pinchole said. "But I'm still very curious about what he or she knows."

"Do what you need to do," the Doctor said, and motioned for Pinchole to follow him. Together they hurried back to the Monitoring Room, eager to hear the latest updates.

Chapter Eleven

DAISHA

Daisha's refuge for the night was a small patch of woods separating two potato fields. A three-quarter moon shined in the night sky; the stars spilled like silver glitter across a never-ending sheet of black construction paper. Back in Palo Alto, before the running, she had always been afraid of the dark. Now, the nighttime world was her best friend.

Using her satchel as a pillow, she rested on a bed of soft pine needles, paranoid about a bug possibly crawling inside her ear. That had happened once while lying in the grass of a Stanford University courtyard. The experience had turned her into a complete insectophobe.

Her thoughts drifted to Axel. Where was he? What was he doing? Was he keeping a safe distance from the Pursuers? A smile came to her lips, remembering the time they had exploded through the Warp and landed in the tiny European country of Liechtenstein. The place was mountainous, quaint, and stunningly beautiful. It had made her feel like she was Julie Andrews in *The Sound of Music.*

"The hills are alive with the sound of reggae!" she had sung in a green meadow on the road to Vaduz Castle, which she later learned was the official home of the Prince of Liechtenstein.

They had lost the Pursuers earlier that morning along a set of railroad tracks in the capital and had made their way up a mountain to check out the castle. The two still had money back then, and they'd stopped at a farm stand to buy picnic food—bread, cheese, strawberries, and two bottles of cold *trink kakao,* the Liechtenstein version of chocolate milk.

As they ate, drank, and basked in the Alpine sunshine, Daisha stared at Axel. His curly brown hair had grown long, draping to his shoulders, and his blue-gray eyes framed with long black eyelashes gleamed in the midmorning light.

In that instant the thought came to her: he's cute.

Axel must have been thinking the same thing about her. As if guided by some invisible force, they looked into each other's eyes, smiled, and held hands. Daisha remembered her heart pounding with both fear and excitement. She had never kissed a boy before, but the urge to peck Axel on the lips burned inside her. But the tender moment had quickly ended when their GeoPorts buzzed, and over the side of a hill trudged the Pursuers and their tenacious, unrelenting solar tracker.

* * *

A series of loud crunching sounds snapped Daisha from her memory.

She sat up on her knees and scanned the darkness. Her senses were on high alert, her muscles tensed to run. There was a long silence, and then more of what sounded like rustling leaves and twigs snapping.

"It's just a deer," Daisha muttered, trying to calm her nerves. "Are there bears in this part of Ohio?"

The thought of a big, stalking black bear sent shivers up her spine. But she knew that bears didn't attack people—unless a mother was defending her cubs. It was June, prime foraging time for mama bears and their babies.

Daisha stood up slowly and slipped the satchel over her shoulders. The line *No rest for the wicked* tumbled into her mind. She had heard the phrase from a head-banging death-metal song on Axel's iPod. That style of music made her brain ache, but Axel loved to crank it up and thrash around like an insane chimpanzee.

"But I'm not the wicked one," she said aloud. "And I still can't get a wink of sleep."

Just then, the GeoPort in her pocket buzzed to life. The vibrations startled her. She slapped at her thigh, thinking at first that a very large insect had crawled up her pant leg. The commotion in the woods grew louder, and she suddenly remembered that the GeoPort only buzzed when...

A man's sweaty, viselike hand reached out of the darkness and grabbed her around the neck. His other arm wrenched around her stomach. Daisha kicked, screamed, and flailed like a fish on the end of a hook. The man's hand clamped tighter on her throat, his other arm squeezing every last bit of oxygen from her lungs.

Her eyes bugged out. She was choking.

"Make a move, and I snap your neck," the man growled in the unmistakable broken English of a Pursuer.

The other Pursuer emerged from the dark woods. He shined a flashlight directly in her face, temporarily blinding her.

"Where's the GeoPort?" he barked. "Tell me now, or we kill you!"

One thought raced through Daisha's mind: How did they track me at night?

She didn't have time to ponder for very long, because the Pursuer's death grip squeezed even harder around her neck.

"You have three seconds to give it up or else!" he shouted in her ear.

Daisha nodded toward the satchel, which the Pursuer had torn from her back during the struggle. It was now lying in the weeds a few yards away.

"In the bag," the Pursuer holding her grunted to the other.

The other Pursuer rummaged through the satchel before dumping its contents on the ground and searching through the items with his flashlight. "It's not here," he muttered.

The hand around Daisha's throat released its grip and checked her pockets.

"Look what I found," the Pursuer said, and wriggled his fingers inside Daisha's pocket.

Daisha leaned forward as far as she could and flung her head backward with all her might. She heard the Pursuer cry out in pain as the back of her skull collided with his nose. She heard the crunching sound of cartilage breaking, and warm blood sprayed out in all directions. Daisha wrestled free from his grip, turned, and kneed him hard in the groin. The Pursuer collapsed to the ground, writhing in agony.

The other Pursuer lunged at her, only to fall flat on his face. A gnarled mass of protruding tree roots had tangled up his feet. Daisha kicked him hard in the head, instantly knocking him out cold.

"I want the solar tracker!" Daisha yelled.

"You mean this?" a voice asked from behind her.

Daisha turned and saw the Pursuer whom she had just kicked in the private parts holding the Oreo cookie-shaped solar tracker.

"Yes," Daisha said. "Give it to me. Now!"

The Pursuer struggled to his feet, blood dripping down his face. "I'll trade you the solar tracker for the GeoPort," he said and then charged at her.

Daisha sidestepped his advance, grabbed his shoulders, and hurled him into the weeds.

The solar tracker fell from his hand. She snatched it off the ground and then raced into the darkness.

Chapter Twelve
AXEL

Axel leaped to his feet, attempting to flee, but he didn't get more than two steps before a very large man pummeled him into the sand.

"Don't move," a voice growled. "Or your life ends here!"

A second Pursuer holding a flashlight approached him from the darkness. For the first time, Axel got an up-close look at two of the men who had been chasing him for the past six months. The Pursuer holding the flashlight was older than Axel had originally thought. Deep lines etched his forehead, and his receding blond hair was graying at the temples. The Pursuer holding him down was much younger, a big and burly man with light-green eyes and a day's worth of unshaven stubble on his chin.

The older Pursuer shined the flashlight directly in Axel's face. "Where's the GeoPort?" he asked harshly.

Axel hacked up a wad of sand that had lodged in his throat. "I threw it in the ocean," he spit out.

"Liar!" barked the younger Pursuer. The man then drilled his knee hard into Axel's chest.

"Owww!" Axel cried out.

"If you don't want him to break ribs," the older Pursuer said, "you will give us what we want."

"I told you," Axel gasped. "I don't have it."

The younger Pursuer slapped Axel hard upside the head. A Fourth of July fireworks show exploded in front of Axel's eyeballs. A loud ringing sensation filled his ears. His stomach heaved like he was about to throw up.

"Search him," the older Pursuer ordered.

"Nothing's here," the younger Pursuer said after searching Axel's pockets.

"It's not in the backpack either," added the other.

Axel's thoughts screamed: Don't search my sock... don't search my sock.

But that was exactly what the younger Pursuer did. He worked his hands down Axel's pant leg until he found the bulge protruding from his ankle.

"Got it!" the Pursuer yelled, holding up the GeoPort for his partner to see.

The older Pursuer tossed his partner a set of flex-cuff

zip ties. "Secure him while I contact Doctor Stain. His rosy face will blush with happiness."

The two men laughed.

The older Pursuer walked down the beach and disappeared onto the boardwalk. The other one grabbed Axel's wrists and cuffed them tightly together. After a moment, his fingers tingled and his hands grew numb.

"These are too tight," Axel moaned. "They're hurting me."

The Pursuer ignored Axel's pleas. Instead, he reached into his shirt pocket and produced a silver flask. They sat under the pier for several minutes. Axel's head ached with the slap, and his hands felt like they were going fall off from lack of blood flow. The Pursuer spent his time slurping from his flask and scratching at what looked like a fresh tattoo of a charging bull on his neck.

Finally, they saw the older Pursuer trekking down the beach in their direction.

"Did you tell him?" the tattooed Pursuer asked.

The older Pursuer nodded. "Yes, and they are all extremely happy. I have a car. Let's get a hotel room. I'm exhausted. The Warp won't reset until tomorrow anyway."

The men lifted Axel from the sand and dragged him to an awaiting red Toyota Camry with a large dent in the front passenger's side door. After tossing him rudely into the backseat, the men sped away through the city streets and onto a four-lane highway. The men referred to themselves by name. Axel learned that the younger Pursuer's name was Loosha, and the older Pursuer's name was Kostia. A large highway sign that said *Welcome to New Jersey, The Garden State* soon came into view.

Tears welled in Axel's eyes. He wondered what they were going to do with him. Torture him, beat him senseless, and then dump his dead body on a desolate country road? Daisha's big smile and pretty round face framed with natty dreadlocks flashed in his mind. They had been apart less than twelve hours, but it already seemed like a lifetime. He hoped that she was safe and not going through what he was.

Loosha shined the flashlight into the backseat. "Don't cry, little baby," he said in a singsong voice. "We are not going to kill you. Doctor Stain wants to do that himself."

Loosha laughed, swallowed from his flask, and then passed it to his partner.

"Give the boy his due respect," said Kostia. "He was cunning prey that took us many months to capture." He took a long swig of the flask and then shouted, "Salute!"

They rode in silence. Finally, after many miles, Axel heard the click of a turn signal and felt the car come to a stop.

"I'll check in," Kostia said. "You stay with boy."

Axel lifted his head and peeked out the window. A large neon sign illuminating the night sky flashed *Edison Plaza Motor Inn—$69 per night*. This was his chance to get away. He tugged and struggled to loosen the cuffs on his wrists and ankles, but they were too tight. The more he attempted to undo them, the deeper the sharp plastic gouged into his bare skin.

Kostia quickly returned and steered the car to a parking spot in front of a row of cheap-looking rooms. Loosha opened the back door, flung Axel over his broad shoulders, and carried him inside.

"Lock him in the bathroom," Kostia said and tossed his partner a roll of silver duct tape. "Cover his mouth with this."

Axel plunked down on the dirty linoleum floor, his face inches from what looked and smelled like a puddle of urine. The man clutched Axel by the scalp with one hand and then duct-taped his mouth and eyes with the other.

"Hope you don't catch cold and get a stuffy nose," Loosha said. "You will suffocate to death for sure."

The bathroom lights went out, a door slammed, and everything fell silent. Axel lay there in the cold darkness, his breathing labored, for the rest of the night. When the Warp reset the next day, he and the Pursuers were hurtling at the speed of light back to the Doctor's headquarters.

Chapter Thirteen

DAISHA

Daisha ran blindly through the dark woods. Low-growing tree branches and bushes spiked with sharp thorns scraped her bare arms and legs. When the trees opened up to blossoming potato fields, she sprinted harder, her arms and legs pumping madly. Only then did she dare to glance backward.

The Pursuers were nowhere in sight.

Of course not, she thought. I kicked the crap out of both of them and grabbed...

Daisha stopped in her tracks. She held the solar tracker up to the moonlight. The thing was no bigger than a silver dollar. It was black, encased in hard metal. A small blue light in the center pulsed every few seconds, illuminating the unit with neon starbursts.

Her GeoPort throbbed to life. She yanked it from her front pocket and noticed that every time the tracker pulsed with blue light, her GeoPort buzzed at the same time.

"That's how those losers track me," she said aloud. "When the tracker flashes, they know I'm close. That means I'm tracking myself right now!"

She reared her arm back and flung the solar tracker into a mucky pond nearby.

"Now you can track frogs and sunfish," she said and started running again.

She didn't stop until the first winks of morning twinkled on the horizon. A gas station and convenience store named Sparky's One-Stop sat on a strip of asphalt between forks in the road. From her hiding place, Daisha watched as a steady stream of hurried commuters stopped to fill their tanks and grab a morning cup of coffee.

A truck delivering fresh baked goods wheeled into the parking lot. The luscious, sugary scent of powdered doughnuts wafted into Daisha's nostrils. Her stomach grumbled with hunger.

Deciding she was safe from the Pursuers even in daylight, she crossed the road and walked into the convenience store. The delivery person was filling shelves. A middle-aged woman with waist-length silver hair was behind the register. Standing in the checkout line were three customers. They all stopped what they were doing and stared at her.

Daisha saw a sign with an arrow next to the milk cooler that said Restroom. She made a beeline toward it and locked the door behind her. Tears burst from her eyes as she gazed at her reflection in the mirror.

She was filthy. Mud and dirt caked her face. Twigs and sticky burrs clung to her dreadlocks. Bloody scratches covered her arms and legs; her clothes were tattered and torn. She turned on the faucet, cupped warm water in her palms, and washed her face.

A knock came at the restroom door.

"Are you okay in there, honey?" Daisha guessed it was the woman from behind the cash register.

"Uh...um..." Daisha stuttered. "I'm fine."

"Well, you don't look fine. Are you with someone outside?"

"No."

"Then do you need me to call someone?"

Daisha let out an exasperated sigh. "I told you I'm fine. I'm just going to the bathroom."

She heard the woman walk away. Daisha spent the next several minutes cleaning her face, hair, and bloody scratches with wet paper towels. She had scrubbed off most of the mud and dried blood, but her clothes were still a grungy mess. Her only other outfit was inside the satchel back with the Pursuers.

"Are you done yet?" a man's voice said through the door. "You've been in there for almost ten minutes."

Daisha opened the door, and her heart skipped a beat. Standing there was a tall, skinny police officer in uniform. Strapped around his waist were a holstered gun, handcuffs, and a baton.

The officer looked at the woman behind the counter. "Is this the one you told me about?"

The woman nodded.

"Have a rough night?" the officer asked Daisha.

"Not really," Daisha answered.

"It looks like you slept in a barn. What's your name?"

"Da...Da...Danielle," she said, not wanting to use her real name.

The officer narrowed his eyes. "Do you live around here, Danielle?"

Daisha nodded her head.

"Where do you live?"

The instinct to run surged through Daisha's body, but she was standing in a small hallway and the police officer was blocking the way.

"Fredericktown," she said, remembering the name from the boy in the cornfield when she had first blasted through the Warp.

"Where in Fredericktown?" the officer asked. "What's your address?"

The blank expression on Daisha's face told the officer all he needed to know. He grabbed her elbow and said, "I think you should come with me." He led her out of the store and into an awaiting police cruiser.

"How old are you?" the officer asked when she slid into the backseat.

"Thirteen," Daisha spit out, deciding that it was no use lying about her age.

A thick pane of shatterproof glass separated the front and back seats. Daisha tilted back her head, closed her eyes, and wondered what would come next. Every muscle in her body ached with exhaustion. All she wanted to do was take a shower, crawl between clean sheets, and sleep this whole nightmare away.

"Hungry?" the officer asked and slipped an English muffin wrapped in aluminum foil into the backseat. "It's an egg, cheese, and bacon sandwich. My wife made it for me this morning, but you look like you need it a lot more than me."

Daisha didn't even take the time to say thank you. She tore open the foil and gobbled down the breakfast sandwich. While she ate, the officer radioed into the police station.

"I picked up a thirteen-year-old girl off of Granville Road who looks in rough shape," the officer said. "She may be a runaway. Get someone from Child Protective Services."

"There's no way I'm going with Child Protective Services," Daisha said through a mouthful of food.

"Excuse me?" the officer muttered.

"Nothing," Daisha quickly answered. "The sandwich is good. Thanks."

She reached down and felt the GeoPort in her front pocket. She had watched a crime show on TV once where the arrested person had to empty out his pockets at the police station. Although she knew the police officer wasn't technically arresting her, he may check her pockets when they got to the station. The Pursuers had almost killed her several times in their efforts to get the GeoPort. There was no way she'd allow a small-town cop to take it from her. She had to find a way to escape. Since the backseat had no handles, opening the door and jumping out of the moving car was not an option. She had to think of something—and fast.

As the cruiser pulled into the police station, Daisha saw her chance. When the officer opened the back door, she'd tear away and run for her life.

A chirping sound came from the GeoPort in her pocket.

Utter joy and relief swelled inside Daisha's heart. Twenty-four hours were up, and the Warp had reset! She could warp out of Ohio to the dog run in Palo Alto. Axel might be waiting there for her. They would be together again!

The coordinates of the Hoover Park Dog Run burned in her memory.

37.4302° N, 122.1288° W

The back door of the cruiser opened. The officer motioned for Daisha to follow him. She took four steps alongside the officer and then tore across the parking lot.

"Get back here!" the officer yelled in pursuit.

When Daisha had a good twenty yards' distance between her and the man, she stopped in her tracks and pulled out the GeoPort.

"She has a weapon!" the officer shouted and reached for his gun.

Her hands were shaking, heart racing. She fumbled nervously with the GeoPort, quickly punching in coordinates. And just as the officer was ready to pounce on her, she pushed the button and detonated into the Warp.

Chapter Fourteen

AXEL

Axel compared a flight through the Warp to leaping off a skyscraper directly into the aurora borealis. Brilliant hues of red, green, yellow, and pink illuminated the swirling tunnel. A plasma tail like from a comet trailed behind him. He felt the tiny bursts of charged particles colliding off one another while the magic of the GeoPort, the solar wind, and Earth's magnetic field transported him to anywhere in the world in a matter of moments.

The only difference between this trip and the others was the company. Instead of sensing Daisha's warm body next to him as they plummeted through the void, he felt the cold, rough hands of the Pursuers gripping his elbows. The fact that Axel's wrists were still handcuffed behind his back made the journey all the more uncomfortable.

An enormous, translucent membrane came into

view. Reflections of brilliant iridescence like a million butterfly wings filled Axel's vision. He felt himself accelerate at supersonic speed toward the light. His stomach lurched, and his brain spun like a top. A solar flare–fueled, geomagnetic blast exploded all around him.

And then he, Loosha, and Kostia punched through the Warp.

"Welcome back to California," Loosha said, wiping beads of sweat off his brow.

They had landed roughly on a large trampoline, and were now bouncing harmlessly up and down, slowly coming to a stop.

"Doesn't look like California to me," Axel said.

"We're in the basement of Hatch Enterprises in lovely Mountain View," Kostia said. "How do you like our landing pad? It sure beats falling directly on concrete or packed dirt."

"I've had better trips."

"You and your little *dziewczyna* have been through the Warp many, many times," Loosha said. "No two trips are alike. Correct?"

"Take off these handcuffs, and I'll tell you."

Kostia tightened Axel's restraints. "We do what Doctor Stain tells us to do. You stay secure until he says otherwise."

“Do you call him Doctor Stain to his face?” Axel asked, remembering meeting the man at his father’s laboratory at Stanford University. Seeing the birthmark for the first time had made him queasy.

Loosha chuckled. “We’re not suicidal. We want to live long enough to spend all the money Dr. Stain will give us for capturing you. There was a five-million-dollar bounty on your head alone.”

“You’ll never get Daisha.”

“From what I have heard on the chatter lines, my comrades have already captured her,” Kostia said. “Unfortunately, it wasn’t us. Our reward money would have doubled!”

Axel’s heart deflated in his chest. He felt sick, scared, and hopeless. Their many months of running were over. The Doctor had finally captured them. The lunatic was moments from having possession of the GeoPort, and an inevitable death sentence awaited them.

The basement door flew open. Two armed guards pulled Axel off the trampoline and led him to an elevator. One of the guards pressed a button, and the elevator lurched upward.

When the doors opened and Axel saw who was waiting for him, he nearly keeled over. There, standing in the waiting room of the most opulent office Axel had ever seen, was the Doctor. The enflamed birthmark on the side of his face was unmistakable.

Deep, unbridled hate of the man instantly boiled Axel's blood. It took every ounce of his willpower not to spit in the Doctor's face.

"Here is the prisoner," one of the armed guards said.

"Remove those handcuffs!" the Doctor scolded. "He is not a prisoner. He is my guest. Take him for a shower and a clean set of clothes. I want him back in my office in exactly one hour."

The guards grunted an apology and led Axel back onto the elevator. Three floors later, they were marching into what reminded Axel of his middle-school gym locker room. There were benches and lockers for changing and storing clothes, sinks, a row of urinals, and some shower stalls.

Axel stepped into a stall and pulled the curtain. He peeled off his grungy clothes, grabbed a bar of soap from a rack, and stepped into the shower. The hot water felt like heaven washing over him. A week's worth of dirt and grime swirled down the drain as he rinsed his hair and scrubbed his filthy body.

He wondered why the Doctor hadn't killed him on the spot. After all, the man now had the GeoPort and had already assassinated Daisha's mother and his father. What else could the Doctor possibly want from him? Thoughts of escape filled Axel's mind, but he knew the idea was futile. The two armed guards were standing feet from the shower stall, their twitchy fingers ready to fire in case of any funny business. He hoped Daisha was washing up too and he'd see her back in the Doctor's office.

Axel turned off the water and stepped out of the shower. One of the guards drew back the curtain and tossed him a towel and a set of new clothes. He dried off and slipped on a pair of clean khakis, a green long-sleeved button-down shirt, socks, and brand-new black sneakers. The guards led him back to the Doctor's office. Daisha wasn't there. It was just the Doctor, a man Axel didn't recognize, and a young woman with blond hair.

"I have dinner waiting for you," the Doctor said to Axel. A sleazy smile stretched across his face. "I can only imagine how famished you must be after such a long ordeal."

Spread out on an oak table in the middle of the room were almost all of Axel's favorite foods—pepperoni pizza, barbeque chicken, pasta salad, and fresh falafel and chicken skewers from Ammar's Hummus Shop. The last thing in the world Axel wanted to do was eat the Doctor's food, but his hunger was too great. He sat down and tore into the chicken skewers.

"Slow down, my friend," the Doctor said. "You'll give yourself a stomachache."

I'm not your friend, Axel thought silently to himself and continued eating.

"My name is Brad Pinchole, PhD," said the man Axel didn't recognize. "I'm the director of Satellite Warp science. I have a lot of questions for you."

"Let the boy eat first," the Doctor said.

"Where's Daisha?" Axel asked.

"She'll be here soon," Pinchole replied.

Axel wiped his mouth and expelled a loud burp. "I want to see her now," he said.

The Doctor and Pinchole shot each other a meaningful look.

"In due time," the Doctor said. "First, we need to speak with you."

"You know the ins and outs of geographical transportation better than anyone," Pinchole jumped in. "I want to know all its bugs, kinks, and ornery sides."

"Why should I tell you anything?" Axel barked. "You've been chasing me and Daisha for six months, trying to kill us just like you did our parents!"

A shocked look washed over the Doctor's face. "Your

parents are not dead. Where did you ever get such a morbid idea?"

Axel stared at the Doctor in disbelief. Could it be true?

"But...I saw them," he stammered. "Your men...shot them in the dog park. Right after our parents gave us the GeoPorts."

"Get his father on the video right away," the Doctor ordered.

Pinchole took out his phone, found what he was looking for, and turned on a large-screen monitor mounted on the wall. On the screen were his father and Daisha's mother in their messy lab in the Varian Physics Building. The two of them were busy working. A young woman with long black hair parted in the middle and icy blue eyes briefly entered the frame. She grabbed a folder off his father's desk and then disappeared from the camera's view. Axel recognized her immediately. Her name was Megan, one of his father's graduate assistants. She had been to his house a few times for dinner and once went on a trip with him and Daisha and their parents to Fisherman's Wharf in San Francisco.

"See, they are right where they are supposed to be, working," the Doctor said. "They have been worried sick and have been diligently trying to find you."

"This can't be," Axel said. "I saw them get shot through the chest. I watched them die."

"What you saw was an unintended consequence of the GeoPorts," Pinchole offered. "We—I mean, your parents—discovered that the GeoPorts produce small levels of deep-space radiation. Too much exposure causes wild, paranoid hallucinations much like a psychedelic drug. You and Daisha were the unintended victims of that mind-altering contamination. Now that the GeoPort is out of your possession, you can see reality clearly."

"Are you trying to say that what happened to me over the past six months was one big mind freak?"

"Not all of it," the Doctor said. "You and Daisha were definitely traveling through the Warp. But everything else was a fantasy. Those men who you erroneously thought were trying to kill you were in reality trying to *rescue* you."

"They work for your parents and Stanford University," Pinchole added. "The Doctor offered to foot the bill to pay for their services."

Axel ran a hand through his long, curly hair, not quite understanding what he was hearing. Could it be true? Had he just woken up from one long nightmare? Was his father still alive, and everything would soon return to normal?

"Then why was I handcuffed?" Axel asked. "Your men gagged me with duct tape."

"Not true," the Doctor said. "Again, this was all part of your radiation-induced illusions."

"But we thought you were trying to kill us."

The Doctor sat down on the couch and draped his arm around Axel's shoulders. "I don't want to kill you. I want you and Daisha to work for me."

"Can I see my dad?"

"Very soon," the Doctor said softly. "I have to attend a Stanford Board of Trustees meeting at the Green Library. Mr. Pinchole has a lot of questions you need to answer about your experiences with the GeoPort."

Pinchole stood up, motioning for Axel to follow him. Together, they left the Doctor's office and into the elevator.

Chapter Fifteen
DAISHA

A distressed whine filled Daisha's ears. Her eyes snapped open. She was lying in a patch of dirt—her head still spinning from the Warp—with a trembling chocolate Labrador cowering nearby.

"Coco!" a voice called out. "Come!"

Daisha quickly stood up. A man in a wheelchair rolled in her direction. He grabbed the dog's collar and snapped on a leash.

"That loud bang scared my dog half to death," the man said. "Did you light a firecracker or something?"

"No," Daisha said.

"Then it must have been those kids riding past on their bikes. Delinquents."

The man and the dog moved away. As the Warp cobwebs cleared, Daisha realized she was inside a fenced-off dog run next to a basketball court. A sign nailed to a tree read Hoover Park Dog Run, City of Palo Alto.

Home.

Happy tears gushed from her eyes from the utter joy of being back in Palo Alto again. She was standing at the exact spot where she and Axel had first flown through the Warp. Below her feet, soaked into the dirt, was a deep red spill of some kind. The jarring memory nearly knocked her over. This was also where the Doctor's men had gunned down their parents.

She quickly scanned the dog run for Axel, praying that his smiling face would emerge from behind a tree. He wasn't there, only strangers and their menagerie of mutts. Afraid the Pursuers might be after her, Daisha hurdled over the fence and ran as fast as she could out of the park.

A weathered flyer attached to a telephone pole caught her attention. There were two photographs of children on the flyer. One was of Daisha, the other of Axel. They were from their eighth-grade Jordan Middle School yearbooks.

MISSING
If you have any information about Axel Jack
or Daisha Tandala, call the Palo Alto Police
Department or the Polly Klaas Foundation.

Someone had torn the rest of the flyer away, but Daisha had seen enough missing persons posters to know that it would list their age, hair color, dates of birth, sex, height, race, and eye color for identification purposes.

The thought of turning herself in to the Palo Alto Police tumbled into her mind, but she quickly dismissed the idea. After all, what would she say to them? She certainly couldn't tell them about the Warp, the Pursuers, and the Doctor. They'd probably toss her into a mental ward.

She hurried down busy Middlefield Road past her old school, and then walked down N. California Avenue to Byron Street. There, in the middle of a row of houses, was the tiny white bungalow she had shared with her mother.

Her heart raced; her breath came in quick huffs. The house looked the same as when she had last seen it six months ago—the tangle of overgrown flannelbush shrubs in the front yard, the garage door that never closed all the way, and the powder-blue shutters in need of fresh paint.

Staked in the front yard was a For Sale sign.

Daisha hopped onto the front porch and tried to open the door. The handle didn't budge. She then climbed over the side gate and went around to the backyard. The kitchen slider that opened up to the patio was unlocked, and she stepped inside. The place was completely empty. All of their furniture, plants, photos, and Caribbean-inspired decor were gone.

"Mom!" she called out, her voice echoing off the bare walls.

When there was no answer, she stepped into her mother's bedroom—empty. A sudden urge to throw up came over her. She ran to the bathroom and heaved into the toilet the half-digested remnants of the egg, bacon, and cheese sandwich the cop had given her. When every bit was out of her stomach, she looked at herself in the medicine cabinet mirror.

Dirt, muck, and filth stared back at her. Lying on the floor next to the sink was a used bar of soap no bigger than a pack of matches. She immediately peeled off her smelly, grimy clothes and jumped into the shower.

Ten minutes later, she felt clean, refreshed, and human again—until she saw the pile of grimy clothes on the bathroom floor.

"I'm not wearing those rancid things ever again," she said to herself, and then stepped out of the shower.

She paced around the house, leaving a trail of wet footprints. From room to room, the memories flooded her brain. The house was now an empty shell. The only thing left of her old life was inside her bedroom closet. Ever since she was old enough to walk, she had collected the sticky bar-code labels from bananas and stuck them on the back of her closet door.

They were still there. Hundreds of them, as fresh as the day she had pasted them. A nostalgic lump formed in her throat. She remembered her secret hiding place. She crawled to the back of the closet and felt for a hole in the drywall the size of a ripe cantaloupe. When she found the opening, she reached inside and yanked out three spiral notebooks filled with her secret thoughts, several pieces of smooth sea glass, a condor feather she had found while hiking Big Sur, and a crumpled pile of red, white, and maroon fabric.

The fabric was the bandanna skirt and ruffled sleeve blouse that her grandmother had sent her from Port Royal. She remembered shoving the outfit into her hiding place so she wouldn't have to wear it anymore. The same dress she was wearing when she'd met the Doctor. Despite that grim fact, she slipped into the skirt and pulled on the blouse anyway. The outfit was tight, but clothes slightly too small were better than wearing filthy rags. After lacing up her dirty sneakers and retrieving the penknife and GeoPort from her old shorts pocket, she was ready to go.

"But there's no place to go," she mused to herself.

She was back in Palo Alto, but Axel was who-knew-where. Their contingency plan in case of separation was to Warp back to the Hoover Park Dog Run. If she and Axel were to be reunited, it would be there.

Daisha left the house and made her way back toward Hoover Park. She stopped at busy Oregon Expressway. Motorists whizzed down the road until the light turned red. Just as Daisha was about to cross, a fancy black Bentley driven by a capped chauffeur screeched to a halt directly beside her. The windows weren't tinted, and she saw a man in the backseat. He had a cell phone to his ear. The man moved his head slightly, revealing a huge red birthmark on his otherwise pale face.

The Doctor.

Daisha froze in her tracks, fear surging through every cell in her body. If she ran, the Doctor would see her. The only chance she had was to stay perfectly still and hope the man wouldn't turn in her direction.

The light turned green, and the Bentley accelerated forward. The Doctor hadn't noticed her! A tsunami of relief washed over until, halfway up the block, she saw the Bentley's brake lights flash and its shiny-rimmed tires screech to a stop.

That was when she ran, sprinting recklessly into oncoming traffic. Car horns blasted as she zigzagged her way across the busy expressway before disappearing into the backyards of neighborhood houses.

Chapter Sixteen

AXEL

Pinchole led Axel off the elevator and into a windowless room. There were a sofa, two overstuffed chairs, a coffee table, a water cooler, and a large television monitor hanging on the wall.

Axel plopped down on the sofa. "I want to see my dad," he said. No matter what the Doctor had told him, Axel wouldn't believe any of it until he could see his father face-to-face.

"Very soon," Pinchole answered and looked away.

Axel noticed that Pinchole couldn't look him in the eye for more than a nanosecond.

"They are involved in very serious, time-sensitive work at the moment," Pinchole continued, his eyeballs darting around the room. "I have immense respect for your father, and Daisha's mother as well. They were two of the finest physicists on the planet."

"You mean *are*."

"Excuse me?"

"My dad and Daisha's mom *are* the finest physicists on the planet. Not *were* the finest physicists."

Pinchole cleared his throat. "Of course, that is what I meant. All of us who work here are looking so far into the future that using the past tense is a bit of a habit."

"Speaking of the past, if I had radiation poisoning from the GeoPort that caused hallucinations, why aren't I in some kind of anticontamination chamber?"

"Once we took the GeoPort away, you were no longer subject to radiation," Pinchole said quickly. "Let's talk about your fantastical experiences using the GeoPort, shall we? I want to know what it was like traveling through the Warp."

"You should already know what the GeoPort is like," Axel said impatiently. "Your men went through the Warp as many times as Daisha and I did."

"Our men were only *following* you through the Warp," Pinchole said. "There is a big difference. Believe me, I would have loved to take a trip myself, but we needed men specially trained in...rescue...so the Doctor only authorized those men for Warp travel."

"Pursuers," Axel said.

"Pardon me?"

"That's what Daisha and I called the men who were chasing us. Pursuers."

Pinchole nodded his head. "Speaking of Daisha," he said, his eyes still unable to look into Axel's, "she should be here in the next day or two. Our men rescued her."

Axel sat up, his pulse racing with excitement. "For real? Where was she?"

"Our men found her wandering in an Ohio cornfield, confused and disheveled, but otherwise unharmed and well."

Twenty-four hours of worrying about Daisha's safety lifted from Axel's shoulders. He missed her desperately, and longed to see her big smile and mop of dreadlocks. But most of all, he wanted to hug her, hold her in his arms, and never let her go again. The word *love* popped into his brain, followed by a strange, fuzzy feeling that tingled through his body.

"As I was saying," Pinchole continued. "We could only follow you through the Warp. That is not the same as you and Daisha logging in coordinates and manipulating the Warp."

"What do you mean?" Axel asked.

Pinchole plucked out his cell phone and held it up. "Let me simplify things. It's the same principle that allows the government to track a person's movements by their cell phone use. Every time you use a cell phone, you leave a cellular footprint wherever you go. You operate a cell phone, and all the government can do is follow you. Get it?"

Axel nodded.

"Now, I want you to tell me everything about Warp travel," Pinchole continued.

"First, where's my GeoPort?"

"Don't worry. We've locked it away inside in the Monitoring Room on the third floor with an armed guard."

"Okay. What do you want to know?"

"Let's start from the beginning."

The beginning for Axel had been at the Hoover Park Dog Run. It was also the end of his father's life—or at least he had thought so. Radiation and hallucinations... Could it all be true? Only when he saw his father alive and well would he be sure.

"I want to see my dad first," Axel said.

"I told you, your father and Daisha's mother are working on a very important project. Your reunion will have to wait."

"My dad hasn't seen me in six months. I find it hard to believe he won't take a minute to see that his only son is okay."

"We've shown you a live video feed of them working in the laboratory. Isn't that enough for now?"

"Please, let me see a live video of them one more time. After that, I promise to answer all of your questions."

A loud groan escaped from Pinchole's lips. "Fine," he blurted and walked over to the television monitor. He fidgeted with the controller until a grainy, black-and-white image appeared on the screen.

The scene was the same as Axel had viewed earlier in the Doctor's office: his father and Daisha's mother inside their messy lab. Then Megan, the graduate assistant, grabbed the folder from his father's desk. He was just about to tell Pinchole to turn off the video when a framed photograph sitting on his father's desk caught his eye. It was of him, taken on school picture day.

Axel hated school photos, but his father always wanted one to keep on his desk at the lab, next to a photo of Axel's mother, who had died when he was less than a year old. A week before Axel had disappeared into the Warp, his father had made a big deal of replacing his old seventh-grade picture with the new one from eighth grade.

"My boy's growing up," he remembered his father cooing.

Axel gazed into the monitor and studied the picture

on his father's desk. In the photo, Axel's hair was short and he had a black eye. The shiner had come from an accidental elbow during a touch football game at recess when he was a fifth grader at Walter Hayes Elementary School.

A ten-ton boulder of realization dropped on Axel's skull in that instant. The half-digested food he had eaten in the Doctor's office angrily belched into his esophagus. A burning sensation filled his throat, and he felt the blood drain from his face.

The picture on his father's desk, and the video feed he was watching, were both over three years old.

Chapter Seventeen
DOCTOR STAIN

"Stop the car!" the Doctor yelled at his chauffeur.

The Bentley screeched to a halt. The Doctor jostled in the backseat, his hot cup of coffee spilling all over his expensive Armani suit.

"What's the matter, sir?" the confused chauffeur asked.

"Did you see that girl?"

"What girl?"

"It was a young black girl with crazy hair. I just saw her run across the street. She looked very familiar."

"Sorry, but I wasn't paying attention."

"Turn this vehicle around. I want to see if we can find her."

The chauffeur wheeled into a driveway, turned the car around, and cruised slowly down the street. There were plenty of people around—joggers, dog walkers, mothers pushing baby strollers—but they didn't see a young girl.

"Recognize anyone?" the chauffeur asked.

The Doctor let out a disheartened grunt. "Not yet. Keep looking."

Daisha Tandala was the spitting image of her beautiful mother. Killing Roswell Jack had meant nothing more to the Doctor than swatting an annoying fly, but ending the life of Jodiann was the most difficult thing he'd ever had to do.

"Take Cowper Street again," the Doctor ordered.

The chauffeur sped up Cowper, down Marion Avenue, and across Waverly Street. The Doctor felt like a spaniel trying to flush a pheasant from the bush. On their second pass down Cowper, he noticed another street called Anton Court. A sign read: *Not a Through Street*.

"Go down that one," the Doctor said. "It's a dead end."

The chauffeur obeyed his boss's command and turned down Anton Court. Only a six-foot hedge separated the street from busy Oregon Expressway. The sound of speeding traffic blasted in the Doctor's ears as memories rushed into his brain. He vividly recalled the day when Jodiann and Roswell had marched into his office, announcing that they were going to dismantle the GeoPort infrastructure and permanently suspend the research. He thought it was a joke at first, but quickly realized the two were dead serious.

When he had asked why, the two fervently spouted some tree-hugger, antitechnology manifesto about the potential misuse of such knowledge. Without using the Doctor's name specifically, they explained that they did not want to be a part of some greedy, multinational corporation that would eventually use the breakthrough for the sole purpose of making money under the guise of *making the world a better place*.

The Doctor had just nodded his head, listening to their impassioned speech with pretend understanding and empathy. When the scientists had left his office, he dialed his cell phone and ordered their immediate assassination. Simply taking the technology for himself and letting the professors live was not an option. They knew too much. The Doctor would not allow them to stand in his way.

"Is that her?" the chauffeur asked.

The Doctor rolled down his window. "Where?"

The chauffeur pointed to the end of the cul-de-sac. There, standing behind a white van was a young, frightened-looking black girl in a red dress with a shock of wild dreadlocks.

She hadn't yet noticed them parked next to the

curb. The girl was taller than he remembered Daisha, but that made sense because he hadn't seen her in six months. And her natty black hair was longer too, more matted and unruly. His first instinct was to jump out, grab her, and make absolutely one hundred percent certain it was really her. But he knew the real Daisha was much more agile and fleet than himself. She was strong, wiry, and adept at escape. If it were really her, she'd bound away the moment he opened the door.

"Inch the car a bit closer," he told the chauffeur. When the car was less than ten yards from her, the Doctor hit Record on the video camera on his iPhone and pointed the lens at her. He then rolled down the window and yelled, "Daisha Tandala!"

The girl immediately snapped to attention. She stared at the car. The Doctor expected her to run immediately, but she just stood there, her mouth hanging open and her eyes wide with confusion.

The Doctor knew that without a doubt the girl was Daisha. She looked just like how he remembered her mother.

A man emerged from the house carrying a large box. He stopped in his tracks when he saw Daisha standing next to the van. "Can I help you with something?" he asked her.

Wanting to diffuse the situation, the Doctor opened the car door and stepped onto the sidewalk. Daisha, seeing that the Bentley was blocking her path back up the street, turned and leaped over a white picket fence and fled into a backyard.

The Doctor made chase. He hurried after her over the picket fence, stepped onto a cedar deck, and looked into the backyard. A dog inside the house was barking. He watched as Daisha scaled another fence and disappeared over the other side. The Doctor ran back to the car.

"She's running toward Marion!" he hollered. "Hurry!"

While the chauffeur sped away, the Doctor frantically dialed the Satellite Warp Lab. Pinchole's mousy mug popped up on FaceTime.

"I want a dozen men on the corner of Cowper and Waverly Streets in downtown Palo Alto in ten minutes!" he roared.

"Why?" Pinchole asked.

"I just saw the girl! She's in Palo Alto!"

"But..."

"Just shut up and get those men here! Start tracking her. There's plenty of sunshine. We've nearly cornered her."

"I'll send the men. But we can't track her."

"Why not?"

"Because the Pursuers trying to capture her in

Ohio just showed up on our doorstep. They're both in pretty bad shape. From what they told me, Daisha kicked the living daylights out of both of them and took their tracker."

"Impossible. She's a thirteen-year-old girl, for crying out loud. Those men are the most highly trained bounty hunters in the world."

"It's true. And without that tracker, we can't pinpoint her location. Each tracker is specific to one GeoPort. Understand?"

The Bentley flew through a red light, nearly causing a collision, and tore down Waverly. The Doctor spotted Daisha again. She had appeared from a driveway and was now sprinting down the sidewalk in the direction of Hoover Park.

"We just got sight of her!" the Doctor exclaimed, nearly hyperventilating. "We'll talk about this later. Forget Cowper and Waverly. I want the men to assemble in Hoover Park. She's headed that way."

He ended the call and gripped the back of the front seat. His knuckles turned white as the car sped in Daisha's direction. The rush to capture the girl was so great that neither the Doctor nor his chauffeur saw the silver Ford Focus ease out of its driveway. The front end of the Bentley rammed directly into the Ford's rear.

Chunks of metal and plastic exploded into the air. The front airbags inflated like giant balloons. Smoke poured from the Bentley's radiator, while gasoline gushed from the Ford's fuel tank.

Within seconds, both cars were on fire.

Hot fumes seared the Doctor's lungs. He struggled frantically to open the car's door, but it wouldn't budge. Fortunately, his window was down and he managed to crawl from the crumpled car into the street. The driver of the Ford Focus, a middle-aged woman with a bloody gash on her forehead, had also escaped the wreckage. Both of them stood there, pale and shaken over the crash.

The chauffeur frantically untangled himself from the seat belt and air bag. He kicked open the driver's side door and escaped just as both cars exploded into a massive fireball. The smell of burning tires and flaming gasoline permeated the air. Onlookers gasped in horror. The Doctor turned and saw Daisha standing among the crowd.

She had witnessed the whole scene.

Chapter Eighteen

DAISHA

Voices cried out.

"Oh my God!"

"Somebody help!"

"Call 911!"

People crossed themselves. Others wept.

Daisha stood on the sidewalk with the shocked crowd. The sight and smell of the two cars burning made her want to throw up, but watching the Doctor stare at her from across the street sent her fleeing back toward Hoover Park.

Police cars, fire engines, and ambulances whizzed past her with sirens blaring. She didn't stop running until she saw the Hoover Park picnic area and collapsed under a shady tree. Her lungs heaved and sweat poured down her temples, the scene of the car crash replaying in her brain on an endless loop. Another thought quickly followed: If only the Doctor had exploded into a fireball, then all of this would be over.

And then her mind turned to Axel.

She sat up, wiped the sweat from her face, and sprinted across the baseball field. Twenty-four hours had passed since their separation in Vietnam. That meant Axel would have put their emergency plan in motion and Warped to the dog run just as she had done.

37.4302° N, 122.1288° W

The latitude and longitude coordinate numbers were more valuable to her than a million-dollar lottery ticket.

A half dozen people milled around the dog run, some tossing balls to their mutts, others sitting on benches texting on phones. There was no sign of Axel. She had no idea where his GeoPort had sent him yesterday. Hopefully, it was a safe and cloudy part of the world so the Pursuers couldn't track him.

But what if he hadn't been so lucky? What would happen to him if the Pursuers followed his trail at night like they had done to her? She had no way of knowing his fate, and that was killing her inside. A roar of car engines caught her attention. Three Hummers raced down Cowper Street and screeched to a stop next to the playground. A bunch of burly men wearing the uniform of the Pursuers stepped out of the vehicles.

She strained to listen as two of the men approached a man pushing a toddler on a swing.

"Have you seen a teenaged black girl with long dreadlocks?" one of them asked.

That was all Daisha needed to hear. She tore out of the dog run, hopped a chain-link fence, and was on the run again. As she ripped across the street, she turned to see if the Pursuers were coming her way. Her chest swelled with relief; they hadn't noticed her.

Thirty minutes later, Daisha was standing in front of the Palo Alto Main Library. She could have gotten there much faster but had decided to skirt far around the scene of the accident to avoid detection by the Doctor's men. She walked into the library, took a long drink from the water fountain, and sat down at a computer station.

"You need to sign up first," a woman behind the lending desk said.

"Huh?" Daisha mumbled.

"If you want to use the Internet, then you need to sign up. You can reserve a computer for one hour. May I see your library card?"

"I don't have one."

The woman raised her eyebrows. "Do you live in Palo Alto?"

Daisha shook her head. "I'm just visiting a friend of my mom's."

"Then you can use a guest pass."

The woman handed her a piece of paper with the login password. Daisha typed in the digits and hit Enter. Google's search engine popped up on the screen. Without hesitation, her fingers pecked out the names *Axel Jack, Daisha Tandala*. There were 80,403 web references to them, as well as over one thousand videos about the *two missing Jordan Middle School students and their murdered Stanford University professor parents*. Nearly every news outlet in the country had run their story. Cable networks like Fox News, CNN, MSNBC, and Investigation Discovery had aired several stories about them.

"We were a national obsession without even knowing it," Daisha said aloud to herself, astonished that with such intense media coverage no one had recognized them, probably because they were mostly outside the country.

She clicked on the first link—a *San Francisco Chronicle Magazine* story titled "Mystery and Murder in Palo Alto"—and started reading. By the time she skimmed past the third paragraph, she realized how far off the police were, along with everyone else. The authority's number one theory was that their parents were part of a Mexican drug cartel. Their killing and the subsequent disappearances of Axel and Daisha were all about drugs and money.

The article showed a picture of their parents' messy lab. A police detective in a jacket and tie was holding bags of white powder and pointing to several jars filled with liquid. The caption under the photo read: *Palo Alto detectives uncover Roswell Jack and Jodiann Tandala's methamphetamine operation in the basement of Stanford University's Varian Physics Building.*

"My mother does not make meth!" Daisha blurted out.

The librarian looked up from her desk. "Quiet, please."

Daisha's cheeks flushed with heat. She sank deeper into the chair and continued reading. Doctor Lennon Hatch's name appeared in the article on page two. The author had praised him for offering a reward of one million dollars for any information leading to the safe return of the two children.

"It was a setup," she hissed under her breath. "The Doctor orchestrated the whole thing to make it look like my parents were making drugs in their lab. Then he made himself look like a freakin' hero."

A ball of hot rage formed in the pit of her stomach. Her muscles tensed; her teeth clenched. She was ready to scream at the top of her lungs when a man looked up from another computer terminal. He was older, with thinning gray hair, deep wrinkles, and slouching shoulders. The man stared at her intently. Daisha realized who he was: Mr. Perry, the retired custodian from her old elementary school.

Daisha's heart froze. She turned away, not wanting to look him in the eye. She was three years older and had dramatically changed physically. Did he recognize her? Not wanting to take any chances, she sat up from the computer and walked by the librarian's desk. She saw a pair of scissors sticking out from a pencil holder. The librarian was busy arranging books in the stacks. As quick as a cat swatting a feather toy, Daisha grabbed the scissors and rushed into the women's restroom.

The dreadlocks that had sprouted from her head since the age of three had to go. The Doctor had seen her with them, and now Mr. Perry was eyeballing her. Tears rolled down her cheeks as she snipped away the first lock. *Snip...snip...snip.* When she was finished, a pile of black hair lay at her feet on the tile floor.

She stared at herself in the mirror. The person

looking back at her was completely unrecognizable. Her mother's face flashed in her mind.

"*Capillum*," Daisha muttered. "The Latin word for *hair*."

Chapter Nineteen

AXEL

Pinchole flicked off the video monitor. "You've seen your father," he said. "He's alive. Now, answer my questions about Warp travel."

Axel leaned back on the couch and rubbed his eyes to keep from crying. The dated video of his father proved that Pinchole and the Doctor were lying to him. Daisha and he were not hallucinating. They had seen their parents assassinated in Hoover Park. The Pursuers were not trying to rescue them; they were trying to capture them.

But Pinchole and the Doctor did not know that he knew the video was old. That was his ace in the hole, a hidden advantage. His only choice was to play dumb and go along with their plans—for the moment.

"The first thing to know about Warp travel is that it sucks," Axel offered.

"In what way?" Pinchole asked.

"Just imagine jumping feet first into an endless hole with the most spectacular special-effects laser show in the world flashing all around you. It's a mind freak."

Pinchole scribbled something on a legal pad. "What do you feel physically during the Warp?"

"Your head throbs, and your stomach flip-flops like a Frisbee tossed by a first grader. Daisha and I have blown chunks a lot of times after flying through the Warp."

"Delightful," Pinchole said with a grimace. "Do you experience any other ill effects?"

Axel shrugged. "Why don't you ask the people who were chasing—I mean, trying to rescue—us about their experience? They went through the Warp as many times as we did."

Pinchole smiled. "Again, our men were only *following* you through the Warp. There is a huge difference between you setting the coordinates and traveling through the Warp, and our men simply sniffing out your trail."

"How?"

"Well, to use the *sniffing* analogy, it's the same thing as a bloodhound using his nose to track a person down. You run through the woods, leaving nothing but footprints and invisible scent particles. The dog just follows those invisible scent particles. It cannot replicate your exact experience of running through the woods. Make sense?"

"I guess so. Now that you have my GeoPort, you can just set coordinates and see for yourself."

A sullen expression washed over Pinchole's face. He scribbled more on his legal pad and then said. "Unfortunately, we cannot use your GeoPort to enter the Warp. We attempted to do that the moment you arrived at our headquarters, but the experiment proved futile."

Axel knew Pinchole would never be able to make it work because of the DNA security coding. To work properly, the scanner on the GeoPorts had to recognize *his* DNA.

"Why?" Axel asked, wanting to hear Pinchole's reasoning.

"The genius of your father and Daisha's mother is why. They somehow programmed the only two GeoPorts in the world to work in tandem with each other. We think that they communicate via highly sophisticated chips embedded in each GeoPort. We have surmised that after twenty-four hours of physical separation, the function of both GeoPorts completely shuts down."

Axel's heart swelled with relief. Pinchole hadn't yet discovered the real reason why the GeoPorts failed to operate.

"You know the twenty-four window for the Warp to reset," Pinchole continued. "That window has passed, and if she hasn't Warped somewhere by now, she isn't going to without your GeoPort."

Axel stood up and glared at Pinchole. "Then just pop down to the Varian Physics lab and ask my father to fix the problem. He's alive, after all."

Pinchole quickly turned away, his eyeballs darting nervously around the room. Axel beamed inside. His ace in the hole had worked perfectly, and he loved watching the lying scientist squirm.

The ringing of Pinchole's cell phone broke the uncomfortable silence. "It's Doctor Stain...Hatch," he mumbled and left the room.

Axel walked over to the door and turned the handle. Locked. His thoughts drifted toward Daisha. What if she was already in Palo Alto, and the Doctor and Pinchole didn't know it? There was no way of knowing. The only thing Axel could do was wait and hope that the Doctor didn't kill him before he could see her again.

He realized Pinchole would never let him die—at least not until the guy figured out that the only thing needed to make the GeoPort function properly was Axel's or Daisha's DNA. Pinchole was a Warp nerd to the utmost degree. Only Axel knew what coordinated Warp travel was like, and that gave him all the power. He could buy time by spooning out Warp facts in little sips and swallows, just enough to keep Pinchole on edge but never telling him everything.

Axel debated giving up one of the Warp's most amazing secrets. The one he and Daisha had discovered while Warping away from Stonehenge in England. They had spent two days in London. When they were able to lose the Pursuers, they visited sites like the Tower of London and Buckingham Palace. On a whim, they had decided to take a train to see Stonehenge, the famous prehistoric megalith. The ancient boulders were huge and, according to the program guide, positioned around 3000 BC with no one knowing for sure who had built the structure. Axel remembered a brisk wind blowing through the stones, making an almost ghostly music. He marveled at how ancient people could have manipulated the fifty-ton rocks without the help of modern equipment. Daisha, on the other hand, didn't care about *how* they made the thing; she wanted to know *why* it was built.

When the Pursuers inevitably tracked them at

Stonehenge, the Warp answered all their questions about the medieval stones.

The moment the Pursuers rushed after them across the Salisbury Plain, they punched matching coordinates into their GeoPorts and exploded into puffs of smoke and electrical discharge. Axel reached out and grabbed Daisha's hand as they tumbled into the ethereal void.

Then they saw something amazing. The normal psychedelic light show of the Warp turned into a series of flashing images. They watched dozens of men dressed in animal skins laying out seven or eight large tree trunks and then rolling a heavy stone along the very same plain Axel and Daisha had Warped from just moments ago. With brute force, the men then lowered the bottom of the massive stone into a predug hole and levered the stone into a standing position.

"That's how they made Stonehenge!" Axel remembered crying out. "Muscle power!"

The images playing before their eyes suddenly hit fast-forward. Stonehenge was now complete. Men in elaborately decorated robes chanted while lifting a deceased man onto a wooden scaffold. Then, with great reverence and high ceremony, they lit the scaffold on fire.

"Stonehenge is an ancient burial ground!" Daisha exclaimed.

They both realized with utter astonishment that the Warp had the power to show them the past.

Chapter Twenty
DOCTOR STAIN

"It may take up to eight weeks for your wrist to heal," the emergency room physician explained. "Try not to get your cast wet."

The Doctor nodded, slipped his arm into a sling, and met two police officers in the hallway of the Standford Hospital emergency room. His statement to them was simple: his chauffeur began to accelerate at a high speed down a residential street, a car suddenly backed out of a driveway, and the cars collided. He could say nothing more. The officers accepted his description of the events, and he was free to go.

News reporters were waiting for him outside the hospital. A massive two-car crash was a hot story on its own, but considering the Doctor's wealth and prestige in the community, the press frenzy was intense.

"I have no comment at this time," the Doctor said

into a microphone that a reporter had shoved in his face. He then slipped into an awaiting limousine and drove away.

The Doctor had never broken a bone in his body before, and despite the prescribed painkillers surging through his veins, his wrist still throbbed. He thought of the lawsuit that would surely follow. The woman in the Ford Focus would be lining up a lawyer to go after a piece of his money. Of course, he knew she would settle out of court. He'd give her a lump sum, and the whole thing would go away.

But the GeoPorts would never leave him. Even with the shock of the accident, his skin tingled with excitement as his plan grew closer to fruition. His men had already captured Axel, and finding Daisha, now that she was in Palo Alto, was just a matter of time.

Pinchole and Kari, the Doctor's secretary, were waiting when the elevator doors opened on his office suite.

"Sir, it's all over the news," Kari said. "Are you okay? What can I do for you?"

"Besides a distal radius fracture, I'm okay," the Doctor said with a wince. He turned to Pinchole. "We need to talk." The two of them stepped inside the office and closed the thick oak door.

"I can't believe this happened," Pinchole said. "How

do you feel? Do you need some time away? I mean, I can handle things."

"Stop blabbering," the Doctor said. "We need to talk about what to do with the boy and how to find Daisha. She's the one who caused this accident in the first place."

"How did she do that?"

"Forget it. How many men are scouring the Hoover Park area for her?"

"Ten. All of them are instructed to take her alive."

"Good." The Doctor sat down at his desk and let out a deep sigh. "They'll find her in short order."

"I was just speaking to the boy before you called," Pinchole said.

"What did he have to say?"

"Not much. He's holding back details. Unfortunately, as I explained earlier, the GeoPorts only work in tandem."

"We may need to play good cop, bad cop a little more with him."

Pinchole raised his eyebrows. "Sir?"

"You must not have watched many detective shows as a kid. Good cop, bad cop is a psychological technique used for interrogation. The bad cop is aggressive, threatening, and nasty to the prisoner; the good cop shows sympathy and support to win the prisoner's trust. It's what I was doing when we first brought him in here. Instead of throwing him into a dark room, I offered him food and hospitality. Get it?"

"Then I'll be the good cop. I'm not very good at being bad."

The Doctor laughed. "That's why I'm a multibillionaire and you're just my right-hand man. I want *Nice guys finish last* etched on my tomb."

"If this were a bad original Hulu series, my canned response would be, 'My dear sir, I'm a man of science and could care less about money,'" Pinchole joked while twisting the cap off a bottle of Coke. "But I love money just as much as the next PhD. However, without the other GeoPort, our research and your business plan grind to a halt."

A jolt of pain shot through the Doctor's wrist. He popped three pain pills into his mouth and washed them down with a glass of water. His face flushed with heat. The port-wine stain on the side of his face pulsed. Dermatologists had managed to lighten the birthmark considerably over the years, but it was still a prominent feature.

"I want you to convince Axel that you want to destroy me," the Doctor said, fanning his face with a manila folder.

"Why would I do that?" Pinchole asked.

"Good cop, bad cop. Tell him that we have Daisha, I'm an evil jerk, and you need their help to stop me. If for some reason we can't capture Daisha—which is highly unlikely—we will lure her into our trap with Axel, the only person she has left in this world."

"But he'll want proof we have her. The old surveillance tape of Professor Jack in the lab has stopped pacifying him. He's asked several times to see his father in person."

The Doctor reached into his pocket with his good arm and pulled out his iPhone. He pressed the camera button to access the video roll and handed the phone to Pinchole. "This should do the trick," he said. "Press Play and see for yourself."

Pinchole watched the video three times, an astonished expression plastered across his face. "This...is... perfect," he stuttered. "It looks like an older version of Daisha. Are you sure it's her?"

"Of course, I'm sure. She looks exactly like her mother."

"Where did you take the footage?"

"While we were chasing her, I filmed twenty seconds of her standing next to a delivery truck. That should be all the proof the boy needs. Now, wring him out until he tells you where to find this Magnes Solace. We still don't know what this mystery person knows. I won't allow anyone else access to this technology."

Using the Doctor's phone, Pinchole texted the video link to his own phone and rushed out the door to show Axel. Good cop, bad cop was about to begin.

Chapter Twenty-One

AXEL

Pinchole burst into the room, ripping Axel from his Stonehenge memory. "I've got good news," he said.

"What?" Axel grunted.

"Daisha. She's back in Palo Alto."

The hair on the back of Axel's neck stood on end, and his skin prickled with goose bumps. "Are you serious?" he blurted out.

"Yes. One of our men just escorted her through the Warp."

Axel's initial excitement over hearing about Daisha quickly turned to distrust. Pinchole had lied about his father, and this was probably another tall tale. The man would do and say anything to trick Axel into giving up secrets of the Warp.

"If Daisha's back in town, then I want to see her," Axel demanded.

Pinchole smiled and pulled a cell phone from his pocket. "Your wish is my command," he said and handed the phone over to Axel.

"What's this for?"

"Proof. Push the play button on the video roll and see for yourself."

Axel pushed Play, and there she was. Daisha's long dreadlocks and lean, muscular frame were unmistakable. She was standing behind a white van with an orange Palo Alto Flowers logo. The footage ended after twenty seconds, and Axel pressed Play again. Seeing her made his heart swell with relief, and he fought the urge to cry. Unlike with the old video footage of his father, Pinchole wasn't lying this time. His best friend was alive and right here in Palo Alto.

"From the emotion written all over your face," Pinchole said. "I can tell a very large weight has been lifted off your shoulders."

"When can I see her?" Axel asked.

Pinchole sat down on the couch next to Axel. "No one knows I took this footage," he whispered. "The Doctor would surely kill me if he knew I showed you this."

"Why?"

"Because he wants to keep you two apart, squeeze out all he can, and then swat you like annoying flies.

The man has no conscience, but I do. I won't let him kill you or Daisha."

The sincerity behind Pinchole's words took Axel by surprise. He didn't know whether to believe him or not. After all, the man had lied to him about his father. Perhaps this was just another bullcrap story. But one fact was indisputable. The video footage he had produced of Daisha was real and recent. Except for the red dress she was wearing, Daisha looked exactly as she had the previous day when they were separated in the Vietnamese café.

"When can I see her?" Axel asked.

"I'd let you see her right now," Pinchole responded. "But the Doctor has other plans."

"What other plans? Now that he has Daisha, both GeoPorts are his. You can travel through the Warp just like we did. You don't need us anymore."

"Daisha's GeoPort was defective when she was captu...rescued by our men. That's one of the reasons you can't see your father right now. He's busy trying to fix them." Pinchole wiped a bead of sweat from his forehead and took a gulp of water. "After the GeoPorts are repaired and working, the Doctor is going to kill you, Daisha, and your parents. But not if I can help it."

Spider-Man: Friend or Foe popped into Axel's brain. It was an Xbox game based on the comic book series.

He had played it obsessively as a sixth grader. In fact, the game had gobbled up so much time that his father made him stop playing. The main plot of the game—besides finding the deadly shards of Venom Symbiote brought to Earth by a meteor—was figuring out whom to trust. Spider-Man's sworn enemies tried to be his friends, and former friends turned into his enemies.

That's exactly what is happening here, Axel's thoughts screamed out. *Pinchole's still lying about my father being alive. He's trying to be my friend, but he's still my enemy!*

Axel's insides gurgled with fury. He quickly swallowed his rage, knowing the game he and Pinchole were playing had to continue. At least until Axel figured out where they were keeping Daisha. Then he and she could escape and figure out a way to keep the GeoPorts out of the Doctor's hands.

"I don't want him to kill us," Axel said. "How can we stop that from happening?"

"Tell me everything you know about Warp travel," Pinchole said.

Axel knew it was his move. If Pinchole was telling the truth, and the Pursuers did not have the same experience as Axel and Daisha during Warp travel, the time had come to give up a secret to keep Pinchole happy.

But what detail could Axel dish out? Warp travel had become as easy as riding a bike. But it hadn't always been that way. On the first few trips, Axel had felt like someone had shoved him into a garbage can and rolled him off the top of a mountain. The ride left both him and Daisha sick, scared, and feeling like their skulls were about to explode. Soon they grew accustomed to the journey, and little by little, they got to know the Warp's amazing abilities.

"You've told me how Warp travel can make you feel nauseous and woozy," Pinchole pressed. "Tell me more. Our men who were trying to rescue you reported that it was nothing but a pitch-black void."

"The Warp's everything but a big, black void," Axel said.

Pinchole's eyes grew wide with excitement. "Keep going."

"It's like jumping into a supersonic rainbow or dancing directly beneath a strobe light on steroids."

"Do you see any images?"

"Lots of them."

"What are they?"

"I'll tell you," Axel said, "if I can see the video of Daisha again."

Pinchole sighed but handed Axel the cell phone. Axel watched the video three times and then handed the phone back.

"I kept my end of the bargain," Pinchole said. "Now it's time to keep yours. I want to know more."

Axel told him about the Warp's ability to show the past. Some images were fascinating, like the time Daisha and he were in Montignac, France, and the Warp showed them prehistoric men painting inside dark caves lit only by firelight. Others were not so pleasant. After Warping away from Salem, Massachusetts, they'd seen Puritans accused of witchcraft dangling from the end of ropes by their necks.

"Fascinating," Pinchole said, a hint of awe in his voice. "Now, tell me about a person who goes by the name of Magnes Solace."

The blood drained from Axel's face. His lungs deflated like Pinchole had just sucker-punched him in the solar plexus. Magnes Solace was their secret contact, the only person who, according to their parents, could destroy the GeoPorts.

"Latitude 23.1483..." Axel mumbled absently, remembering the partial coordinates Daisha's mother had spit out right before the Doctor's men murdered her.

"Latitude what?" Pinchole asked. "Did you just garble latitude coordinates?"

Axel shook his head. "Nothing. I've never heard of anyone named Magnes Solace."

Chapter Twenty-Two

DAISHA

Daisha was a stranger to herself.

Without her hair, she felt exposed like an exotic, long-haired Persian cat shaved to resemble a hairless sphynx. The smells of the crash still lingered inside her nostrils. She splashed cold water on her face, trying desperately to cleanse herself of the sense memories.

A soft rap came on the bathroom door, startling Daisha so much she nearly leaped out of her shoes.

"Are you okay?" The librarian's voice echoed through the door. "You've been in there for fifteen minutes, and other patrons need to use the facilities."

"Um...I'm...okay...Just one minute," Daisha stuttered, and then scooped the mound of dreadlocks off the floor and shoved them into the garbage can. She looked at herself one last time in the mirror and then charged from the bathroom, heading straight for the library's exit.

"I have to get back to the dog run and look for Axel," Daisha said to herself once she was outside.

The Doctor had seen her, and she knew his men were crawling all over Hoover Park and Palo Alto looking for her. Maybe they wouldn't recognize her. She looked like a completely different person without dreadlocks, someone much older. She could maybe even pass as a Stanford University freshman.

Or Magnes Solace.

Who are you? Daisha wondered. Why did Axel's father tell us to take the GeoPorts to you? And what's an electron diffusion region?

Electron. Diffusion. Region.

The three words just popped into her head, and it took her a moment to remember where she had heard them before. Her mother had said them moments before the Doctor's men killed her and Axel's father. Her frantic, hushed voice echoed in Daisha's ear as clearly as the horrible moment she had spoken them—*Only the electron diffusion region can destroy them.*

Daisha leaned against a tree, carefully analyzing the words. "Only the electron diffusion region can destroy them," she muttered. "Take them to Magnes Solace."

The tight sleeves of her Jamaican-style bandanna

dress dug into her armpits. Daisha reached up and yanked at the fabric, trying to stretch the openings. She remembered her mother's words when she'd given her the dress.

Her mother had said something like, "My dear *solis,* go put on the *decorus vestio* your *avia* sent..."

"*Decorus* means lovely or beautiful in Latin," Daisha whispered to herself. "*Vestio* has to mean dress, and *avia* is obviously the word for grandmother. I'm not quite sure about *solis,* but it sounds a lot like *Solace.*"

The connection hit her. "Could what we thought was *Solace* really be *solis* in Latin?" she exclaimed. "*Magnes* might be a Latin word too!" She gave a quick tug on the hem of her constricting dress and then rushed back into the library.

The librarian glared at Daisha as she signed up for one of the computer stations.

"Are you the same girl who was just here?" the librarian asked, staring at Daisha with bewilderment. "Your hair...It's...gone."

Daisha mumbled something incoherent, grabbed a pass, and sat down at the same computer she had used before. Mr. Perry gawked at her cross-eyed like he had just seen a ghost. Daisha didn't care. She pulled up Google Translate, configured the search to convert

Latin to English, and typed in the word *Magnes*.

"Magnet," she said under her breath. "*Magnes* means magnet in Latin. What about *solis*?" She typed in the word, and nanoseconds later the translation appeared on the screen. "Sun. *Solis* means sun. Magnet sun...sun magnet...magnet of the sun."

Mr. Perry sat up from his computer station and approached the librarian. Daisha watched as they spoke with each other. From their hushed tones and intense stares in her direction, they were obviously discussing her.

Daisha quickly typed the words *magnet of the sun* into the search field. The first hit was a Wikipedia entry for something called the Konanavlah Sun Temple in Madhya Pradesh, India. Ancient rulers had built the temple in the tenth century in honor of the Sun God, Surya. After skimming the rest of the entry, Daisha clicked on the next link—a website dedicated to ancient man-made temples.

The website discussed the mysterious and mystical qualities of ancient temples around the world. Daisha clicked open the page dedicated to the Konanavlah Sun Temple. The engineers who designed the temple had used the principals of magnetism. Before falling into ruins, the peak of the temple was a massive fifty-ton magnet. This was so that a statue of an ancient sun deity, also constructed of magnetic material, could float in midair. The site of the Konanavlah Sun Temple was supposedly one of the most magnetic places in the world.

"Interesting," Daisha mused. "But does it have anything to do with my mother, Axel's father, and GeoPorts?"

She then typed *electron diffusion regions* into Google. The first of more than fourteen million search results piqued her interest. The entry was an article from the UK Space Agency—Britain's version of NASA—titled "Gateways Hiding in the Earth's Magnetic Field." She clicked open the website and read.

> Electron diffusion regions, also referred to as X-Points, are places in Earth's magnetic field that connect to the sun's magnetic field. This creates a clear warp portal from our atmosphere to the sun.
>
> Scientists tell us that these magnetic warps open and close several times each day where Earth's geomagnetic field meets the solar wind. "The only problem is that we can't predict where one will be," says Oxford University physicist Graham Alderson. "Warp portals are sneaky buggers

> because they open and close without rhyme or reason. Rumors are flying around the scientific world saying that two American physicists from Stanford University have discovered a permanent X-Point, but nothing has been proven as of yet."

Latitude 23.1483, the partial coordinates her mother had managed to spit out, flashed in Daisha's mind. She quickly typed *Konanavlah Sun Temple latitude longitude* into the search field and hit Enter. The first hit nearly made her pass out on the library's carpet.

23.1483° N, 79.9015° E

Konanavlah Sun Temple Coordinates

"Magnes Solace isn't a person!" Daisha cried. "It's a place *and* the electron diffusion region my mother was talking about!"

The librarian, who was still watching her intently, quickly picked up the phone at the front desk. "Nine-one-one," she said, "this is Kelly Marston at the Palo Alto Main Library on Newell Road. There's something very strange going on with one of our patrons."

Daisha didn't wait around to hear what the librarian said next. She dashed out of the library, tears of joy and relief gushing down her cheeks.

Chapter Twenty-Three
DOCTOR STAIN

A steady dose of prescription painkillers numbed the Doctor's wrist pain. The wounded, helpless feeling that accompanied it made him feel like a child again. He sat back in his comfortable office chair, remembering the merciless teasing he had endured during his school years. A big oaf bully named Chucky Simmons had called him Stain for the first time during a fifth-grade gym class. The awful nickname stuck all the way through Mount Whitney High School in Visalia and beyond.

One particularly embarrassing moment had Chucky serenading him, out of tune and at the top of his lungs, to the howling high-school lunch crowd. The bully had sophomorically changed the words to "Purple Haze" by Jimi Hendrix to Purple Stain.

> Purple Stain all over his face!

Must be a freak from outer space!
Stain's mutated mug makes me wanna hide!
'Scuse me while I cover my eyes!

Years later, the Doctor finally had the last laugh. When the eight-hundred acres of Central Valley farmland that had been in Chucky's family for five generations went into foreclosure, the Doctor swooped in and bought the sprawling property. He then bribed several members of the Visalia City Council to rezone five hundred acres of the land from agriculture to commercial. When the Tulare County Sheriff served Chucky's family with a final eviction notice, the Doctor was there to witness the teary-eyed scene. The Doctor Lennon Hatch Shopping Mall and Conference Center now stood where Chucky and his ancestors had once grown almonds and pistachios.

A copy of the *San Jose Mercury News* sat on the Doctor's desk. The crash was still front-page news. Not caring to read about his own misfortune, the Doctor flipped open the local news section and skimmed the police blotter. Tricycles stolen from a preschool in Sunnyvale; Burlingame caller reports a naked man walking down the street wearing a donkey mask; woman arrested after kicking Walmart employee; transient arrested after stealing purse from an unlocked vehicle; suspicious African American female snips off dreadlocks in bathroom and flees Palo Alto Main Library.

The last entry made the Doctor's heart stop. His men had been scouring Hoover Park and Palo Alto looking for Daisha. Was the suspicious African American female in the library really her? Did his men overlook her just because she had cut off her hair? These questions whizzed through the Doctor's brain as he picked up his phone and dialed Pinchole.

"The boy just told me an amazing tidbit concerning the Warp!" Pinchole gushed as he stepped into the Doctor's office suite ten minutes later. "He claims the Warp has some kind of psychic ability to see directly into the past. If that's true, then maybe it has the ability to see into the future!"

"Fascinating, I'm sure," the Doctor said. "But I didn't call you up here to talk about him." He handed Pinchole the newspaper. "Read today's police blotter."

Pinchole mumbled aloud. "Suspicious African American female...snips off dreadlocks...flees library. It has to be her!"

"It's absolutely her. Our men are looking for a striking young black girl with long dreadlocks. If she's cut off her hair, they could have easily passed her on the street without even realizing. Can we get a likeness of her?"

"She was last seen in the Palo Alto Main Library. The library has digital video security cameras. A couple years ago, there was a lot of controversy over the installation of those cameras—a potential affront to intellectual freedom, privacy issues, and that kind of stuff. I can get someone to easily hack into their security system and retrieve footage of the girl. That way we will have an exact likeness of her."

The Doctor smiled. "Perfect. We'll pick her up by the end of the day. I wonder what she was doing at the library. Using the computers for Internet access?"

"That's easy enough to find out. Hacking into a public library patron's web-surfing habits is easy."

A loud chanting blasted outside the Doctor's office window. He stood up from his chair and peered outside. A couple hundred protestors, waving signs with sayings like *Google = Evil* and obnoxiously pounding bongos, were marching outside Googleplex. The Doctor couldn't help but chuckle. The activists were mostly college-aged kids with a sprinkling of gray-haired ex-hippies. To the outside world, Google was an innovative, cutting-edge technological leader, and to some, one to be feared. The Doctor knew otherwise. When he got his hands on the second GeoPort, he would tower over Google, Royal Dutch Shell, BP, and everyone else on the Forbes top ten list of most powerful companies in the world.

The Doctor drew the window shade. "What other *tidbits* did the boy reveal to you?" he asked Pinchole.

"For one thing, he knows nothing of the mysterious Magnes Solace," Pinchole answered. "Or so he says. I told him we already have the girl. He'll want more proof she's alive to give up anything else."

"Does it really matter?"

"Sir?"

"Now that we know she has altered her appearance, our men will pick her up soon enough. We'll then have the second GeoPort and won't have a need for Axel."

Pinchole shrugged. "This is true, but I'd still like to squeeze information from him. In a geographical transportation sense, he's the equivalent to Neil Armstrong, the first human to walk on the moon. Plus, if he inherited any of his father's tremendous genius in physics and mathematics, he'd be a great asset to our organization—after a thorough indoctrination, of course."

The Doctor shook his head. "I don't want him around for any longer than is necessary. When we pick up the girl, I want him disposed of in good order."

"What do you mean by *disposed of*?"

The Doctor shot him a you-know-exactly-what-I'm-talking-about expression.

Pinchole nodded. "What about the girl? Get rid of her too?"

"Absolutely not," the Doctor said. "She's brilliant just like her mother. With the proper indoctrination, the girl could serve us well in the future."

Before Pinchole could respond, his cell phone rang. "Yes," he said, answering. "I'm with the Doctor right now. What do you mean, the security camera went down? You have to be kidding me! Then lock everything down and secure the building. I'll be down in a second."

"Tell me what's wrong," the Doctor demanded.

Pinchole hung up the phone, his face ashen. "It's the boy. He's escaped from his room."

Chapter Twenty-Four

AXEL

The shocked expression on Pinchole's face when Axel told him about the Warp's ability to see into the past was priceless. The man's eyes grew as wide as softballs, and his lips quivered. He then jumped out of his chair and paced around the room.

"Must be something to do with photon acceleration...solar wind...traveling faster than the speed of light," Pinchole mumbled excitedly. "This could change everything!"

"Now let me see Daisha," Axel demanded. "I gave you something. Now it's your turn to give me something."

"Yes...right...of course. But she's with...um...a medical doctor right now."

"Why does she need a doctor? What's wrong?"

"Nothing's wrong. Remember? The Warp subjected both of you to small amounts of radiation that caused hallucinations. She's just getting a clean bill of health from a medical professional, that's all."

Pinchole's cell phone rang, interrupting their conversation. "I'm on my way," he said to the caller and then hung up. "I'll be back shortly. What you told me was absolutely mind-blowing. I can't wait to talk more!" He raced out of the room, slamming the door behind him.

Axel heard the *click-click* sound of Pinchole locking the door. Everything fell silent except for the pounding of his captor's nerdy Converse sneakers (emblazoned with a hand-drawn Batman logo on the toes) running down the hall toward the elevator. Axel took a swig from a water bottle and glanced up at the security camera mounted high on the far wall. The glass eye was watching his every move. As he capped the water bottle, he noticed a sliver of black on the otherwise white ceiling. One of the tiles in the drop ceiling was askew, as if someone had taken the handle of a broom and accidentally popped it out of place.

What's up there? Axel wondered.

He looked closer and saw a ventilation shaft. He remembered watching a character in a science fiction movie escape from an alien spaceship by wiggling his way through something similar.

The ceiling could be his way out, but he'd have to

cover up the camera lens. The person on the other end would surely see him and send up an alert. He knew he just couldn't walk over and throw a T-shirt over the lens. How could he disable the camera without anyone suspecting he was doing it on purpose? The answer came to him in an instant.

Sock Football.

The game Axel used to play by himself every football season popped into his thoughts. He was a hard-core 49ers fan and loved watching the games every Sunday while playing Sock Football at the same time. The football was just a bundle of dirty socks knotted into the shape of a ball. He was the quarterback. After dropping back to pass, he'd fire the ball to a wide receiver from across the living room. The wide receiver was a wicker basket tucked into a corner. If the ball landed in the basket, it was a touchdown. If the ball bounced onto the couch or recliner, it was an interception. After Axel broke two living room lamps and a handblown glass figurine of a hummingbird, his father had made him quit.

Maybe I could play a game of Sock Football and accidentally break the camera, he thought. He knew that a balled-up sock would not disable a surveillance camera, but a Nike sneaker probably could do the trick. He quickly took off his shoes and placed the small wastebasket in the corner directly below the camera.

It was time to put on a show.

"I'm bored!" he said loudly, convinced there were also microphones hidden in the room. "I miss playing football. I wonder how the 49ers will do this year. Okay. I'm the quarterback. If the shoe lands in the wastebasket, it's seven points. Down...set...hut...hut!"

Axel reared back, pretended to elude a pass rusher, and then fired the sneaker toward the basket. "Score!" he shouted, raising his arms in the air. "Axel Jack to Jerry Rice for a touchdown!"

The game continued like this for five minutes, with each successive throw getting closer to hitting the camera. Finally, Axel cocked his arm, aimed, and flung his sneaker as hard as he could at the intended target—a direct hit. The heel of the sneaker smacked violently against the camera's wall mount, causing the lens to crack and the bracket bolts to loosen. Without support, the entire unit crashed to the floor.

Not wasting a millisecond, Axel slipped on his shoes and positioned a chair under the crooked ceiling tile. He jumped up, using his fist to punch open the tile. Cautiously, he reached up and felt for a handhold. Two firm steel rods ran along the ceiling. He hoisted himself through the hole and into the ventilation shaft. Utter blackness engulfed him. After replacing the tile, he crawled army-style.

The space was tight, barely big enough to fit his frame, and clogged with so much dust that his eyes watered and his nose tickled with an imminent sneeze. Then his shirtsleeve got stuck on something. He looked down and saw that it was caught on a jagged piece of metal sticking up between two sections of the shaft. After a quick tug, his shirtsleeve pulled free of the metal, but not before ripping off a huge hunk of the fabric.

A claustrophobic cocktail of anxiety mixed with fear clawed at his thoughts as he wormed his way through the maze of ductwork. Sweat poured from his temples, and his heart pounded with adrenaline. Just when he thought he'd be crawling in the tunnel forever, he saw light.

Bars of golden sunshine filtered through a series of grille slats in the wall. Axel wriggled another ten yards and peered through the openings. He smelled fresh air and saw a jacaranda tree in the distance. The vent led to the outside, and the drop was an easy ten feet to a delivery loading dock. Using his closed fist, he pounded at the grille, trying to pop it open. The thing didn't budge. He ran his hands along the casing, hoping to find a weakness. A loose bolt on the bottom left corner offered a glimmer of hope. Using his thumb and index finger, he removed the bolt and pressed with all his might. The bottom half of the grille slowly gave way, but not enough for him to fit through the opening.

"I could probably kick the vent open with my feet," Axel mumbled. "But I'm headfirst. How am I going to turn around?"

A chorus of muffled voices echoed down the shaft from the room he had just fled. One of them was Pinchole, for sure. The man had discovered him missing, and now his goons were hot on the trail. Axel rolled on his side, bringing his knees to his chest. The goal was to force his feet forward and upper body backward. His legs would then be in the correct position to kick out the grille.

The pressure of the tight space was intense. His head throbbed, and his breath came in quick huffs. On a silent count of three, he twisted like a freak show contortionist before finally flip-flopping into the correct position. He then kicked at the grille with all his might. After several big blows, the barrier peeled away and crashed to the pavement below.

Axel shimmied from the shaft and fell to the ground, every sense on high alert. He heard chanting and the sounds of drums and tambourines. He peeked around the corner of the building and saw a massive compound with a sign that read *Googleplex—1545 Charleston Road 847*. Hundreds of marchers were staging some kind of protest out front.

They were his ticket to freedom. He rushed into the center of the crowd and disappeared out of sight from his captors.

Chapter Twenty-Five

DAISHA

Daisha spent the next day living like a great horned owl. She slept during the daytime in her empty old house (a real estate agent showing the property had almost caught her snoozing on the living room floor) and waited until night to hunt Axel. She figured a reversal of a normal schedule made her safer from the Doctor's men, who were still scouring the streets looking for her.

The hack job she had given herself in the library bathroom still felt weird. Her scalp was constantly dry, itchy, and flaky like she had the world's worst case of dandruff. She had scratched at her head so much that dried blood caked her fingernails. Along with her hair, the two-sizes-too-small bandanna dress was now gone, compliments of a Salvation Army clothing drop on Pulgas Avenue in East Palo Alto. There she had ripped open a plastic bag and found a pair of pink sweatpants and a faded Cal Poly Mustangs T-shirt. The new duds had a musty smell and were a little too big, but they would do.

Nearly two days had passed since she and Axel had frantically Warped away from the Vietnamese café. Where he'd landed was still a mystery to her, but one thing was certain: if Axel was alive, he'd eventually Warp back to the dog park.

"Shut up!" she barked at her own thoughts. "Axel's alive and well, and I'll see him soon."

Her attempt at self-reassurance didn't work. Tears rolled down her cheeks, and for the first time she imagined a life without Axel. The times they had spent Warping around the world filled her thoughts. She remembered soaking in a thermal pool in Iceland and watching the hypnotic northern lights; touching the crumbling marble ruins of the Roman Forum in Italy; riding the Wiener Riesenrad giant Ferris wheel in Vienna.

As day melted into night, Daisha left her house and crept up the moonlit sidewalk. All of her senses were on high alert. Every person walking or jogging down the street was a potential Pursuer. The headlights of slowly cruising cars were the bright eyeballs of the Doctor on the hunt. Still, she headed straight to Hoover Park.

The park was completely empty when she arrived there. She slipped over the chain-link fence surrounding the dog run and took position behind the trunk of a large tree. Here she waited patiently in the quiet darkness, praying for Axel to materialize through the Warp.

An hour later, a barking dog broke the silence.

"Boris, settle!" a man shouted in broken English. "*Cichy, chłopak*! I'll spend the rest of my time off training you if I have to!" He then kicked the dog hard in the ribs to stop its barking.

Daisha's heart pounded, and she instantly regretted coming back to the park. She peeked from behind the tree and saw the figure of a tall man open the gate of the dog run. He was holding a leash attached to a large black-and-white dog with pointy ears and a bushy tail curling in a ring over its back. The accent was very familiar to her. Either it was an international Stanford student from an eastern European country, or it was a Pursuer. She hoped it was the former. The man and his dog moved within ten yards of her. She watched as the dog lifted his back leg and took a pee. Every ounce of her being wanted to run, but if she moved a muscle, the man and dog would notice her for sure.

There was the sound of a dog leash unsnapping. Two seconds later, the animal sauntered over to the tree where Daisha was hiding, took another pee, and then started to bark at her. She made a motion to run, but the man grabbed her from behind.

"Where are you going, my sweet *dziewczyna*?" the man whispered in her ear, his hot breath foul with cigarette smoke. He flicked on a small penlight and shined it in her face. "Ha! I knew it was you, Daisha. You thought cutting your hair would fool us."

"Let me go!" Daisha cried out. "You're hurting me."

"Shut up! I'm going to turn you over to Doctor Stain for a very large amount of *pieniądze*—cold, hard cash."

Daisha tried to get away, squirming and kicking with all her might, but it was no use. The man was too big and strong.

"You're a fighter, *dziewczyna*," the man said, clamping down on her windpipe. "But not tough enough. You know, I was the one who shot your mother right through the heart in this very spot."

Fireworks danced in front of Daisha's eyeballs. The blood vessels in her cheeks exploded under the skin. The black-and-white dog barked again, this time louder and more aggressively than before. She heard a loud crack. A spray of warm blood flicked across her face. The Pursuer screamed in pain. His fingers loosened around her neck, and then he collapsed into a limp heap on top of her.

A rush of lifesaving air filled Daisha's lungs. She gasped and pushed the heavy man off her. She sat up on her knees, taking deep breaths and wondering what had just happened. The Pursuer was lying unconscious in the dirt with a bloody gash in the back of his skull. The once-vicious dog was now cowering against the chain-link fence, tail between its legs.

"Are you okay?" a male voice asked from the darkness.

Daisha's first instinct was to run, but the fight with the Pursuer had sapped all of her energy. All she could do was kneel in the dirt, massage her aching neck, and wait for what was going to happen next.

"Who are you?" she whimpered. "What do you want?"

The person who had clubbed the Pursuer stepped out of the shadows. He was holding a bloody tree branch the size of a baseball bat.

"Axel," Daisha whispered through shredded vocal chords, and then she collapsed unconscious into the dirt.

Chapter Twenty-Six

AXEL

Axel didn't recognize the girl in the darkness, nor did he hear his name escape from her lips right before she passed out. He only saw that she was young and dark-skinned, with short hair and wearing pink sweatpants.

"Are you okay?" he asked, kneeling next her. The steady rising and falling of her chest indicated that she was alive. He gently patted her cheek. There was no response. Movement from the black-and-white dog caught his attention. The animal trotted sheepishly over to the man who had attacked the girl, gave his bleeding skull a sniff, and then urinated all over his face.

A chortle escaped from Axel's lips, but he quickly suppressed the laughter, knowing the seriousness of the situation. Seeing that the dog was no longer dangerous, Axel walked over to the man he had just bashed into the dirt and felt the side of his neck. There was a light pulse.

"Thank goodness I didn't kill the guy," Axel said under his breath. He then took a good look at the man's bloody and dog pee-soaked face. There, etched on the man's neck, was a familiar-looking charging-bull tattoo.

"It's that filthy pig, Loosha!" he hollered, and instantly his memory flashed back to the young Pursuer wresting him into the Coney Island sand, duct-taping his mouth and eyes, and then locking him inside a dirty bathroom.

An urge to unzip his fly and take his own pee on the man's face briefly crossed Axel's mind. He thought better of it and turned his attention to the girl. What should he do with her? Perhaps find a pay phone and call 911 so they'd send cops and an ambulance. He noticed a few items scattered on the ground. One was a small handgun that the Pursuer must have dropped when Axel clubbed him over the head. Then he noticed something small, black, and round lying in the dirt. When he scooped it off the ground and realized what it was, he nearly passed out right along with the girl.

"This has to be Daisha's GeoPort!" he screamed.

Uhhh..." A groan escaped from the girl's lips as she stirred.

Axel quickly ran to her. He plopped down beside her and cupped her face in his hands. The dreadlocks were gone, but the shape of her lips and cheekbones were as familiar to him as his own reflection.

"Daisha!" he cried. "It's me, Axel!"

Her eyes blinked a few times and then opened completely. A weak smile stretched across her face. "I found you," she said softly.

Axel pulled her to a sitting position and wrapped his arms around her. "I missed you so much. What happened to your hair?"

"A long story," Daisha said, hugging him back.

Just as Axel was about to kiss her, a large, dirty fist swung out of the darkness and clocked him square in the face. Axel fell away from Daisha, pain searing through his jaw. Still dazed from her battle, Daisha struggled to her feet. Loosha stared menacingly at her, his angry face streaked with sweat, blood, and dog pee.

"I'm going to kill you!" he growled.

Daisha tried to run, but her legs were too weak to move. Loosha jumped at her. Just as he was about to grab her, the black-and-white dog leaped out of the darkness. Loosha cried out as the dog drove its sharp fangs into his forearm. Axel struggled to his feet and saw the same tree limb he had used before. He quickly swiped it off the ground, swung with all his might, and bludgeoned the man into submission once again.

Axel crumpled to his knees, his chest heaving and his jaw throbbing.

"Is your mouth okay?" Daisha asked.

"I can talk so it's not broken," Axel said, rubbing his face. "I'm sure it'll just be sore for a while."

A set of high beams shining in the distance caught their attention. They watched as a tan Hummer with tinted windows slowly cruised down Cowper Street toward the park.

"We have to get out of here," Axel said. "But where can we go?"

"Let's go to my old house. It's empty right now. That's where I've been hiding out."

"Perfect. The Doctor's men will be swarming all over this park any moment."

They hustled ten yards to the dog run exit, and then Axel abruptly stopped in his tracks. He turned and looked at the dog, who was again cowering next to the chain-link fence, whimpering.

"Come on boy, girl, or whatever gender you are," he called out. "If it wasn't for you and those sharp canines, who knows what would have happened to us."

"I overheard the guy calling the dog Boris," Daisha said.

"Boris, come," Axel ordered, and then added a quick whistle. The dog perked up his ears and trotted over, and all three of them disappeared into the dark city streets.

Chapter Twenty-Seven

DOCTOR STAIN

The Doctor flung back his head and howled with laughter.

"Excuse me, sir," Pinchole said. "But what's so funny?"

"Your facial expression," the Doctor said, wiping away a tear. "You look like you just saw a ghost."

"The boy just escaped from his room. I think we all should be a little concerned. How could he have possibly gotten out?"

"The security camera should give you a clue."

"Our guy on the other end of the camera said there was a malfunction. When he went to the room to investigate, the boy was gone."

"Idiot! You probably forgot to lock the door."

Pinchole pointed to his skull. "I have OCD. I absolutely locked that door and checked it four times. I'm heading to the basement to look for myself."

"Hold on a moment," the Doctor ordered. "We're not finished talking."

A deep sigh escaped from Pinchole's lips. He ran a hand through his thinning hair and sat down on the chair. The Doctor poured himself a drink and then fired up a Gurkha Black Dragon, the most expensive cigar in the world.

"Our men are on high alert so the boy won't go far," the Doctor said, exhaling a puff of thick smoke. "We have his GeoPort. The thing is locked up safe and secure, right?"

"Absolutely," Pinchole answered, fanning the air in front of his face. "It's locked up in a cabinet inside the Monitoring Room with a twenty-four-hour security detail. It would take the Army Special Forces to pry it away."

The Doctor picked up the *San Jose Mercury News* and scanned the police blotter again. "'Suspicious African American female snips off dreadlocks in bathroom and then flees Palo Alto Main Library,'" he read aloud. "Without a doubt the 'Suspicious African American female' is Daisha."

"I'd say that is a ninety-nine percent certainty," Pinchole said. "We'll get a good image of her without hair and circulate it to the men. I recently hired a girl named Stiv who's freakishly adept at the art of hacking. In fact, she's so good the guys in the lab nicknamed her Stiv the Hacker."

"Also, see if Daisha was using the Internet. I want to know her search history."

Pinchole nodded, dialed his cell phone, and told the woman on the other end of the line what to do. "She'll have everything we need shortly," he said, hanging up the phone. "Now, please, can we head to the basement and figure out how that boy escaped from his room?"

The Doctor popped two more prescription pain pills and washed them down with his drink, and then he and Pinchole hurried down the hall to the elevators. When the doors opened on the basement floor, two guards holding assault rifles and one highly trained, female Belgian Malinois dog were standing inside the room.

"The little rodent broke the camera," the Doctor said, looking at the smashed surveillance equipment lying on the floor.

"The door was still locked from the outside," one of the guards said, holding up a key.

"I knew I didn't forget to lock the door!" Pinchole exclaimed.

The Doctor stepped over the broken camera equipment and looked around the room. "Unless that boy has the power to pass through solid objects like some comic book superhero, he found a way to escape from inside this room."

The guard held the couch cushion that Axel had been sitting on to the dog's nose. After deeply sniffing the fabric, the dog explored the space, tail wagging and muzzle to the floor. When the dog got to a spot in the far corner of the room, she barked and began jumping high in the air.

"What's wrong with that mutt?" the Doctor asked.

"She found the boy," the guard answered. "He must be hiding in the ceiling tiles."

Pinchole smiled. "I knew the kid couldn't have gotten very far." He stepped under the ceiling tile and shouted, "Axel! We found you! Come on down before we sic this dog on you!"

There was no response.

"Get him down from there," the Doctor barked impatiently. "I'm tired of these games."

The guard dragged over a chair, used it as a step stool, and punched out the tile with his nightstick. He poked his head through the space. "Nobody's up here," he said, his voice muffled. "It's just a ventilation shaft that leads into the...Wait...I think I found something."

"What is it?" Pinchole asked.

"Looks like it's nothing," the guard answered, sliding back out of the ceiling. "It's just a piece of green fabric or something."

Pinchole grabbed the fabric from the guard and examined it closely. "This is from Axel," he said. "It's the color of the green shirt he was wearing. That little worm is wiggling his way to freedom through the ventilation shaft."

"Get in there after him!" the Doctor ordered.

The guard attempted to climb farther into the shaft but only got as far as his shoulders. "It's way too small," he said, climbing back out.

"The shaft must lead to the outside," Pinchole said. "Get a ring of men to surround the building. Now!"

The two guards and the dog hurried out of the room and sprinted down the hallway. The Doctor stepped cautiously onto the chair, mindful of his broken wrist, and poked his head into the ventilation shaft. He flicked on a small penlight and peered inside. Cobwebs and dust filled the space. He wondered why anyone—even a desperate, terrified boy—would try to escape through a tight, constricted, claustrophobic corridor like this one. The irony of the situation did not escape him. Axel had eluded him for half a year by slipping into a phantasmagorical passageway, and now he was escaping again through another dark tunnel.

Pinchole's phone rang. His ringtone was the theme song to the old 1960s Batman television show. For some reason, the Doctor found the song incredibly annoying. He lowered himself out of the shaft, brushing the dust and debris from his expensive suit jacket.

"That was fast, Stiv," Pinchole said into the phone. "Great. I want you to make fifty eight-by-ten posters of her without hair, and I'll pass them out to our security team. Yes, of course I want to know what she was googling during her time in the library. Magnet of the... huh? Konanavlah Temple...what?"

"What are you mumbling about?" the Doctor asked.

"Whoa...Stop right there!" Pinchole gasped. "Stiv, I want you to repeat what you just said very slowly. She searched for the words *electron...diffusion...region...*" Pinchole lowered the phone from his ear and looked at the Doctor, a stunned expression on his face. "Sir, we need to see Stiv ASAP. It seems Daisha was googling some very unusual search terms. All of which should be well beyond her realm of knowledge."

Chapter Twenty-Eight

DAISHA

Daisha and Axel hurried through the dimly lit streets with Boris trotting right along with them. Daisha's house was normally only a fifteen-minute hike from the park, but this trip took twice as long because they had to constantly dive for cover whenever a car whizzed down the street. While they walked, Axel told Daisha all about his capture and subsequent escape from the Doctor's headquarters.

"Now they're looking for both of us again," Daisha said.

"Except this time I don't have a GeoPort," Axel remarked.

"Are you telling me the Doctor has your GeoPort?"

Axel nodded. "We don't have to worry until they figure out that only my DNA will make the thing function properly. Which is bound to happen sooner than later."

A jolt shot up Daisha's spine when Axel unexpectedly reached out and held her hand. Their fingers intertwined, and her initial surprise quickly turned into something warm and comforting. Only two days had passed since their separation in Vietnam, but to Daisha it felt like a year. She didn't let go of Axel's hand until they had reached her house.

They slipped into the yard through a side gate. A rustling sound near the back of the yard made Boris bark an alarm.

"Shush!" Axel ordered, and they stepped into the house through the unlocked kitchen slider.

The house was pitch-black. Daisha fumbled through a drawer next to the dishwasher and pulled out a candle and lighter. With a flick of her thumb, she touched the flame to the wick until the empty dining room glowed with a dancing orange light. Boris investigated the place with his nose and then plopped down on the hardwood floor. Daisha and Axel sat cross-legged next to the candle, gazing into each other's eyes.

"You look really funny without your dreads," Axel said.

"Better watch it, big guy," Daisha retorted, punching him playfully in the arm. "Or I just might snip off those flowing curly locks while you're asleep."

"That might not be such a bad idea."

"What do you mean?"

"The Doctor and Pinchole know me with long hair. If I chop off my hair like you, they may not recognize me on the street."

"Who's Pinchole?"

Axel ran a hand through his hair, trying to imagine life without it. "He's the Doctor's main geek. His ringtone is the theme song to the old Adam West–era *Batman* TV show."

Daisha laughed. "The guy must not be that bad."

"Pinchole's bad, all right. He's obsessed with our parents' work and the Warp. He'd probably sacrifice his own grandmother to get my GeoPort to work for him."

A blast of wind rattled the windowpanes. Boris's ears perked up. He let out a bark followed by a low growl. Daisha stood up and looked out the window. After seeing nothing, she walked over to the sink and filled a paper cup from a stack left by the real estate agent. Boris lapped up its contents in a few quick slurps.

"He was thirsty," Axel remarked.

"Do you want something to drink?" Daisha asked.

Axel shook his head. "They fed and watered me well while in captivity."

Daisha's stomach grumbled. The last thing she had

eaten was from a sample cheese plate while wandering around Whole Foods the day before. A stack of papers sitting on the kitchen counter caught her attention. They were listing sheets and a notice of an open house for this coming Sunday.

"The Realtor must have been in the house earlier this evening," Daisha said. "If they sell this place, we need to go somewhere else."

"Where will we go?" Axel asked.

"India."

"Do you mean the country or the Amber Elephant Restaurant on West El Camino Real?"

A big smile stretched across Daisha's face. "The country."

"You have a good time sightseeing. I can't go. Remember, I don't have my GeoPort anymore. We each need our own to go anywhere."

Daisha grabbed one of the Realtor's listing sheets and a pen. She sat close to the candlelight and wrote *23.1483° N, 79.9015° E.*

Do these coordinates look familiar to you?" she asked.

"Not really," Axel replied.

"They are the latitude and longitude coordinates of the Konanavlah Sun Temple in Madhya Pradesh, India."

"Is that place supposed to mean something to me?"

A lump formed in Daisha's throat, a dam of tears ready to burst from her eyes. "Right before they killed my mother, she managed to say a partial coordinate—Latitude 23.1483..."

"You're right! It's where we can supposedly find this mysterious Magnes Solace person to destroy the GeoPorts!"

"Only Magnes Solace is a place, not a person. And it's not *Solace*. It's *solis* as in *s-o-l-i-s*. *Solis* is Latin for sun. *Magnes* is Latin for magnet."

Axel sat up and paced around the kitchen. "That day my dad told us to 'take them to Magnes Solace.' I just assumed Magnes Solace was a person."

"I thought the same thing. Then I remembered all the Latin my mother taught me."

For the next ten minutes, Daisha explained her findings. How electron diffusion regions—or X-Points—were unstable hidden portals that connected Earth's magnetic field to the sun's magnetic field. Their parents had discovered a predictable X-Point, and that precise location was the Konanavlah Sun Temple. The Sun Temple, also known as the Magnet of the Sun, was supposedly one of the most magnetic places in the world.

"Don't you get it?" Daisha said. "The first half of the

Sun Temple's coordinates is 23.1483°. Konanavlah Sun Temple...Magnet of the Sun. Our parents would have explained the same thing if only they had lived another five minutes."

"Everything you said makes perfect sense," Axel said, astonished with what Daisha had just laid out for him. "The Sun Temple is where we can destroy the GeoPorts. But how can we do it?"

"I guess we'll have to figure that out when we get there."

"You mean, when *you* get there. I'm staying put right here in Palo Alto until I can get back my GeoPort from the Doctor."

"Okay. Let's go get it then."

"No, you have to go to the temple without me," Axel said. "If the Doctor captures both of us trying to steal back the GeoPort, then we can't do anything to stop him. Warp to India tomorrow morning. Get the lay of the land and see if you can figure out how we get rid of the GeoPorts forever."

"I don't want to leave you again," Daisha said, her eyes growing misty.

"Same with me, but there's no other way. I've been inside the Doctor's lair. Pinchole let it slip that they were keeping my GeoPort in the Monitoring Room on the third floor. I'll figure out a way to sneak back in and get it. When I do, I'll Warp to India and then we can be free."

Without another word, they collapsed into each other's arms, holding each other until the chirping fox sparrows in the backyard signaled the morning sunrise.

Chapter Twenty-Nine

DOCTOR STAIN

The Doctor and Pinchole met Stiv the Hacker inside a private conference room next to the Monitoring Room. She was young and fresh from UC Berkeley's computer science program. Nerdy yet hip retro glasses framed her face, metallic blue hair sat in spikes on top of her partially shaved head, and a conga line of silver studs dangled from her ears. Colorful tattoos of exotic flowers and mystical creatures decorated her upper right arm.

After introductions, they huddled around her laptop, eager to see what she had uncovered concerning Daisha's search history.

"I already told you over the phone that Daisha searched the term *electron diffusion region*," Stiv said, "She also played around with Google Translate. She was particularly interested in translating Latin to English."

"Who, besides the Pope, has any use for Latin?" the Doctor wondered.

"What words was she trying to translate?" Pinchole asked.

"*Magnes* and *solis*. *Magnes* means magnet, and *solis* means sun."

Pinchole slapped a palm to his forehead. "Holy mother of Moses, Solace and *solis* sound exactly the same! Magnes Solace may not be a person after all! What else was she looking for?"

"She then googled the words *magnet of the sun*. The first hit was a place called the Konanavlah Sun Temple in India." Stiv looked up from her laptop. "Didn't they film scenes from an old Indiana Jones movie there?"

The Doctor let out an impatient sigh. "What does a temple in India have to do with anything?"

Stiv shrugged. "Don't know. But she spent over seven minutes reading the page, so it must have been important to her."

"Let's slow down and figure out why the Konanavlah Sun Temple so piqued her interest," Pinchole said, scratching his chin. He pointed to the article on-screen. "It says here the place is supposedly one of the most magnetic places in the world. This is very intriguing, if I do say so myself. Magnes Solis...magnet of the sun.

Temple...magnetism. Electron diffusion region."

"I can see the neurons inside your brain firing up," the Doctor said. "Are you connecting the dots?"

"Her final search was *Konanavlah Sun Temple latitude longitude,*" Stiv added. "The answer Google gave her was 23.1483° N, 79.9015° E."

With Stiv's words, Pinchole's knees buckled slightly. His face turned white. He grabbed the back of a chair to keep from falling over. "The girl did it," he huffed. "She may know...where..."

"Stop blubbering like an idiot!" the Doctor barked. "What are you trying to say?"

"I'm saying that a thirteen-year-old girl quite possibly figured out this puzzle and not me, a man with a PhD and dual majors in both physics and mathematics from Stanford University."

"You should have gone to UC Berkeley," Stiv joked. "Then you could have figured out whatever the heck you're talking about long ago."

"Pinchole, you have about three seconds to start making sense," the Doctor demanded.

"X-Point, X-Point, X-Point!" Pinchole shouted, shaking his fists in the air. "Don't you get it?"

Stiv leaned over and whispered in the Doctor's ear. "I think he's losing it."

"What the hell's an X-Point?" the Doctor asked.

"An electron diffusion region is sometimes called an X-Point," Pinchole explained. "They're places where the sun's magnetic field connects with Earth's magnetic field, creating a kind of portal in the atmosphere. We erroneously thought Magnes Solace was a person. Daisha figured out that Magnes *Solis* is a place—the Konanavlah Sun Temple, the Magnet of the Sun!"

The Doctor felt his stain flush with intense heat. Every ounce of his being wanted to run to the bathroom and dunk his head in cold water. Instead, he rushed over to the small refrigerator in the corner of the room, took out a cold bottle of water, and held it to his flaming face.

"Ignore me," the Doctor said. "Finish what you were saying."

Pinchole looked at Stiv. "Do you want me to continue with her in the room? I mean, this is top-secret stuff I'm about to reveal."

"Do you trust her?" the Doctor asked.

"I guess, but..."

"Then I trust her. Besides, she's smart enough to know how powerful I am."

"This is all falling into place," Pinchole continued, his voice squealing with excitement. "Daisha is a prodigy. She definitely inherited her brilliant mother's brains, but I digress. As I have explained to you many times, geographical transportation works like this. We use big space magnets to capture the electrons found in the solar wind. Then we transfer the electrons to Earth via infrared lasers. The enormous energy gives us the ability to dematerialize the elemental composition of the human body to a stream of charged particles. GeoPort units then reconstitute those particles back to human form and transfer them to any latitudinal and longitudinal point on Earth. I now realize the GeoPorts only work because of an uninterrupted opening of an X-Point—an electronic diffusion region. Are you following me?"

"Wow," Stiv said. "This is absolutely amazing. Keep going."

"I know all about the scientific mumbo jumbo," the Doctor said. "Please, get to the point."

"The point is that the Konanavlah Sun Temple is a predictable X-Point!" Pinchole shouted. "Professors Jack and Tandala discovered one of these elusive openings, which made the Satellite Warp and geographical transportation possible. We don't need Axel, Daisha, or the GeoPorts. Now that we know where we can find an X-Point, we can make our own GeoPorts!"

“Both of you are getting the cart way before the horse,” Stiv said.

“What do you mean?” Pinchole asked.

“You can’t expect to waltz over to India with a team of scientists and start messing with a revered holy site from the tenth century.”

The Doctor laughed.

“Did I say something funny?” Stiv asked.

“Not at all,” the Doctor said. “You just reminded me that I’ll need to take my checkbook along when we go to India.”

“You might have to grease quite a few fingers to pull this off,” Pinchole added.

The Doctor turned his attention to Stiv. “Since you know so much about our project, I want you to come to India with me as my personal assistant. What do you say? A girl of your talents will be a great asset to our operation.”

“You ask me like I have a choice in the matter,” Stiv said.

The Doctor smiled. “I like the way you think. Enjoy the ride. You are about to have a front-row seat on the greatest technological advancement and business venture the world has ever known.”

“I wouldn’t miss it for anything,” Stiv said, a

flirtatious hint in her voice.

"I'll need at least a week to assemble a team and all of the equipment we'll need," Pinchole said.

"You'll be ready in three days," the Doctor ordered and walked out of the room.

Chapter Thirty

AXEL

Axel and Daisha slipped out of the house and ran in the direction of the Palo Alto Animal Shelter. Boris trotted along with them, stopping every so often to sniff a tree trunk and then mark his territory with a squirt of pee.

"This is a big mistake," Axel grumbled, his eyes darting back and forth on the lookout for Pursuers.

"I will absolutely not leave Boris to run the streets and possibly get hit by a car," Daisha said. "Or worse, have his previous owner, that disgusting Pursuer, take possession of him again."

"Whatever. He's just a dog. Someone would have noticed him roaming around without a collar and then taken him to the shelter. It doesn't have to be us."

A second later, Boris made a beeline for a soggy, half-eaten bagel lying in the gutter. The dog chowed it down in three quick bites. Watching Boris eat made

Axel realize how hungry he was. He couldn't even imagine how ravenous Daisha must be. When they finally hooked up, she mentioned that she hadn't eaten since the day before. That means almost two days had passed since her last bite of food.

"I'm starving," Axel said. "I wish I had some money."

"Please, don't mention food," Daisha said, patting her grumbling stomach. "It just makes me sad."

"I could try shoplifting a candy bar or something from the 7-Eleven."

Daisha gave him a cross look. "Are you crazy? All we need is for you to get busted stealing a Snickers or Kit Kat."

Axel nodded. They jogged in silent hunger until the Palo Alto Animal Shelter came into view. There were no cars in the parking lot, so they stepped up to the entrance. A large sign read: *Only residents of Palo Alto, Los Altos, and Los Altos Hills may surrender animals here. DO NOT leave pets outside of shelter when we are not open.*

"Looks like we're breaking rule number two," Daisha said.

"We'll have to find something to tie him up and get out of here fast," Axel said. "If a Hummer full of Pursuers cruises by, we're dead meat." He rummaged through a garbage bin and pulled out a long piece of shredded twine caked with black grease.

Using skills learned from Boy Scouts, Axel made an overhand knot on one end of the rope, pulled the other end through the loop, and slipped it over Boris's head. He then secured the dog to a bicycle rack.

"Boris isn't going anywhere," Axel said. "Let's get out of here. This place is too wide open."

"It's hot," Daisha said. "I'm not leaving him without water."

Axel groaned. "Do you want to get caught? It's almost seven thirty. The sign says the shelter opens at nine. People will get here soon. He'll be fine."

"I wish you could come with me, boy. But I don't know if a dog could physically handle a trip through the Warp."

"Besides that, only your DNA will make the GeoPort work," Axel added. "The dog couldn't go through even if he'd be fine."

Boris whimpered and bit at the impromptu leash, his otherworldly dog sense telling him that they were about to leave.

"Let's fly," Axel said. "I don't feel safe here."

Daisha stroked the dog's head, tears running down her brown cheeks. With Axel going back to the Doctor's lair in search of his GeoPort and her Warping to Madhya

Pradesh, India, and the Konanavlah Sun Temple, they both realized that there was a very good chance they would never see each other again.

"Don't cry," Axel said, reassuring her. "We'll be together in India before you know it."

A red Toyota Corolla with a missing hubcap wheeled into the parking lot. Axel and Daisha instantly shot to attention, unsure if they should run away or stay put. Before they'd agreed on a plan of action, the driver pulled the car into the handicapped spot directly in front of them. A middle-aged woman with shoulder-length brown hair and glasses turned off the engine, stepped out of the car, and limped over to them, assisted by a silver cane. She was wearing a white T-shirt that said *DOG IS MY COPILOT* in big capital letters.

"Can I help you with something?" the woman asked.

"We found this dog roaming the streets," Axel answered, his heart pounding in his chest.

"He didn't have a collar or anything," Daisha added, wiping away tears.

The woman bent over and let Boris sniff her fingers. "Fine-looking animal," the woman said. "I can tell by his black-and-white markings, pointy ears, and curly tail that he's a purebred Karelian Bear Dog. They're extremely rare outside of their native

Finland. What's more unique is that the dog still has his blue puppy eyes. They usually turn dark brown after six weeks or so."

"You're right," Daisha said, studying Boris's eyes. "I never noticed before. Actually, they're more violet-colored.

"What's a Karelian Bear Dog?" Axel wondered.

"They're bred to hunt large game like moose and wild boar. The breed is also famous for protecting its owner from bear attacks. That's where its name comes from. In fact, the Karelian Bear Dog is so naturally ferocious that park rangers in Yosemite sometimes use them for bear control. Where'd you find him?"

Axel and Daisha answered at the same time, but with different answers.

"Hoover Park."

"Byron Street."

"Well, what is it?" the woman questioned with raised eyebrows. "Hoover Park or Byron Street?"

"He was running on Byron Street, and then we took him to the Hoover Park Dog Run to see if his owner was there," Daisha said quickly.

"I see," the women said. "He could just be lost and not homeless. If we find an animal running the streets without tags, we put an ad in the pet section of the newspaper to see if anyone will claim it before officially putting it up for adoption. The person who paid a pretty penny for this Karelian will most certainly be on the lookout for him."

The woman punched a series of numbers into the security pad, and the front door clicked open. "Please, wait right here," she said. "We don't officially open for another hour or so. Let me take a few minutes to get settled, and then I'll put him right into the quarantine cage so our vet can check him out."

"What do we do now?" Daisha asked when the woman disappeared inside the building.

"We carry on with our plan," Axel said. "I'm going to get my GeoPort, and you're going to India. The shelter will take care of Boris."

"But what if they put an ad in the paper and that Pursuer who you knocked silly claims him?"

"Against my wishes, you forced us to bring the dog to the shelter. That's all we can do."

"Okay," Daisha said. "But I want to stay with him awhile before Warping to India."

"Do what you need to do, but don't wait around too long. Wish me luck. After I get back my GeoPort, I'll see you at the Konanavlah Sun Temple."

"Do you remember the coordinates?"

Axel smiled. "23.1483° N, 79.9015° E." He wrapped his arms around Daisha, hugged her with all his might, and then ran down the sidewalk.

Chapter Thirty-One

DAISHA

Daisha watched Axel vanish down the street. Her best friend leaving, combined with dumping Boris off at the shelter, made a lump form in her throat. The dog lifted his muzzle and let out a series of distressed howls, as if calling Axel back to them. It was of no use. Axel was gone, and now it was just the two of them.

"Me and you and a Karelian Bear Dog named Boris," Daisha hummed, remembering the tune of some obscure song she had once heard on the radio but changing the lyrics to fit her present situation.

The hot morning sun blasted full force right in Daisha's face. Boris was panting, his pink tongue flopping from the side of his mouth like a flimsy slice of bologna. A shady seating area ran along the side of the building. She untied Boris from the bike rack and led him to a bench. Instantly, the temperature dropped a good ten degrees.

"Good boy," Daisha cooed and then slipped the leash from around his neck. "I don't think you need this. You aren't going anywhere."

Boris barked and then returned Daisha's act of kindness by licking her cheek.

"Doggy kisses!" Daisha gushed and then wiped away the saliva. "For some reason, I can't see you charging after a grizzly. Then again, considering the way you tore into that Pursuer who was trying to kill me, you really are fearless."

A loud car engine roared from behind the shelter. Daisha ignored the commotion until she heard two car doors open and then slam shut.

"Henrik, tell me again why we are looking for this dog?" a deep voice grumbled.

"It is the least we can do for Loosha," Henrik said, his voice thick with a foreign accent. "He is laid up in the hospital after that beating he took. Plus, he paid two thousand dollars for that stupid animal. I told him paying that much for a dog was a complete waste of *pieniądze*."

"The moron went on a spending spree the moment he got the bonus from Stain for capturing the boy," the other man added.

Henrik laughed a high-pitched squeal that made Daisha's skin crawl. She perked up, her ears straining to hear the rest of their conversation.

"The dog has a GPS chip inserted under the skin," Henrik said. "My device says we are very close."

"With any luck, someone found the mutt on the street and dropped him off at this shelter," the other man said. "We'll claim him and then go looking for the girl, hopefully getting our own fat bonus."

Before Daisha had a chance to digest what she had just heard, the two men turned the corner. They stared at her and Boris. Henrik held up a GPS device. The thing was beeping like a smoke detector whose battery was about to die. The other man pulled a crumpled piece of paper from his pocket. He studied the paper for moment, looked at Daisha, and then back down to the paper.

"It is Boris," Henrik said. "We have found him."

"It's also the girl with her hair cut!" the other man exclaimed. "She looks just like the poster Pinchole passed out to everybody!"

Daisha didn't wait around to hear another word. She turned and sprinted through the parking lot as fast as her weary feet could take her, Boris chugging right along with her. The sound of the men's hard-soled shoes pounded behind them in hot pursuit.

"Stop!" Henrik yelled. "Or I will shoot!"

Boris turned on the men. The dog pinned back his ears, let out a vicious-sounding snarl, and leaped at the gunman. Daisha heard the sound of bones crunching as Boris's powerful jaws clamped down on Henrik's wrist.

"Ahhh!" Henrik cried in agony, dropping his handgun on the hot asphalt. "Shoot him! Get this dog off me!"

The other man reached into his jacket pocket, yanked out a pistol, and fired. The bullet missed its mark. Boris lunged at the gunman, sharp fangs and viselike jaws ripping into his calf. The dog's sudden attack made the man lose his grip on the pistol. The firearm hit the asphalt and skittered out of reach. The woman from the shelter limped out of the building, frantically screaming into a cell phone.

"Get animal control and an ambulance here immediately!" the woman ordered the person on the other end of the line. "There's a dog attacking two people in the parking lot of the Palo Alto Animal Shelter!"

Daisha, who had been watching the scene unfold from across the street, yelled for the dog. "Boris!" she hollered. "Come! Let him go! Come, boy!"

Boris was at first reluctant to let go of the man, but soon he gave in to Daisha's pleas and ran to her.

Together, as sirens blared in the distance, the two of them headed back in the direction of Daisha's old house. When they finally got to Byron Street, Daisha saw a silver BMW sitting in the driveway. A sign spiked into the front yard and decorated with colorful helium balloons read:

OPEN HOUSE
10-1
Tommi Lawson Realty

Daisha plopped on the curb, head in her hands. The tears came strong and hard. Loud, heaving sobs that lasted for several minutes. When the weeping had run its course, she hugged Boris around the neck.

"You and I are a lot alike, my friend," she said, stroking the dog's chin. "Bad men are tracking you too. Several of whom are crawling every inch of Palo Alto looking for us at this very moment."

A well-dressed blond woman, probably Tommi Lawson herself, stepped out of the house and walked to her car. She grabbed a black briefcase from the front passenger's seat and returned to the house.

"What am I going to do with you, Boris?" Daisha wondered.

She knew taking the dog back to the shelter was out of the question. After what he had done to the Pursuers in the parking lot, the authorities would euthanize him for sure.

"You're going to have to fend for yourself until I can come back and find you," she said, stroking the dog's back. "It'll be easy since you've got that GPS chip embedded in you."

Daisha stood up and wiped tears from her face. The time had come to warp to India. She pulled out the GeoPort and typed in the coordinates for the Konanavlah Sun Temple—23.1483° N, 79.9015° E. Boris went crazy. He jumped on her, whimpering and whining, begging her not to leave him.

"I know you don't want me to go," Daisha said. "I want to stay with Axel too, but I..."

The idea suddenly came to her. She would not leave Axel after all. She immediately deleted the coordinates to the Konanavlah Sun Temple and typed in a new set of numbers. Ones that she remembered looking up for no particular reason at an Internet café in Ho Chi Minh City a couple days earlier—37.4220° N, 122.0840° W.

With the press of a button, an explosion of smoke and electrical discharge blasted in Daisha's face, and she evaporated into the Warp.

Chapter Thirty-Two

DOCTOR STAIN

The Doctor, Pinchole, and Stiv stood inside a private airplane hangar at the Santa Clara County Airport. They watched as several muscular men loaded containers of materials into a rented Boeing 747 Large Cargo Freighter.

"That is the biggest plane I have ever seen," Stiv said. "It looks a beluga whale on steroids."

"The thing's a little too large if you ask me," the Doctor remarked. He turned to Pinchole. "Is it really necessary for us to bring all these materials?"

"It's absolutely necessary," Pinchole said, scrolling on his iPad. "They just loaded a Bjorn 800 MHz nuclear magnetic resonance spectrometer. The container before that was an extremely powerful x-ray laser used to measure the atoms in plasmas."

"Why would we need to measure blood?" the Doctor asked.

Pinchole stifled a giggle. "Not that kind of plasma, sir. We measure *cosmic plasma* made of electrons, protons, and ions. Earth's magnetic field is like a protective shield, protecting us from the solar wind's constant stream of cosmic plasma radiated from the sun. All this is how Professors Jack and Tandala created geographical transportation and the actual GeoPort units."

The Doctor shrugged. As far as he was concerned, Pinchole was just counting the trees. He, on the other hand, was seeing the entire forest. The world around him was going about its normal business, but what he was on the verge of accomplishing was anything but. The Doctor Lennon Hatch Geographical Transportation Company was about to make its final breakthrough, and the Doctor could barely contain his excitement. He figured that they were less than a year from starting up the wealthiest and most powerful company the world had ever known.

"I want to thank you again for inviting me along," Stiv said to the Doctor. "Just a year ago, I was a new computer science PhD from UC Berkeley and now I'm working for you, the fourth-wealthiest man on the planet."

The Doctor smiled, the birthmark on his face flushing bright red at the younger woman. "Soon to be number one, I guarantee you. You know, the moment I laid my eyes on you, I knew there was something very special about your lovely face. You are just the kind of unique individual I want on my team. Play along, and you will be in for the ride of your life."

Stiv's fingers reached up and stroked the Doctor's hand. "I'm here for the long haul. And you will soon find out I'm a terrific team player."

"By the way, where did you ever get the name, Stiv?"

"The Dead Boys."

"Excuse me?"

"A guy named Stiv Bators was the leader of a seventies punk band called the Dead Boys. My parents were hard-core punk rockers in their youth and named me after him."

The massive roar of an airplane engine interrupted their conversation. The Doctor looked up and saw the Boeing 747 lurch forward and roll its way out of the hangar.

"Don't tell me you need another cargo plane," the Doctor grumbled.

"Not at all," Pinchole reassured him. "We managed to get everything we needed on one plane. Also, thanks to you *persuading* the local Indian officials, we have an entire building at a local private school. It's only a few hundred yards from the Sun Temple, plus we get meals and lodging at their staff quarters."

"I bet they make an awesome vegetarian tikka masala," Stiv said.

Pinchole shot her a hard look and then turned to the Doctor. "Sir, can we speak in private to go over some final details?"

"Fine," the Doctor said. "Stiv, you might as well go home and pack. We leave tomorrow morning bright and early."

Stiv smiled and left the hangar. The Doctor and Pinchole watched her walk away.

"She's a very charming young lady," the Doctor said. "I sure never thought I would say that about a girl with blue hair, tattoos, and multiple piercings."

Pinchole blushed but didn't respond.

"I think you have a crush on the girl," the Doctor teased.

"Yes, she's easy on the eyes," Pinchole said. "Most of the guys in the Monitoring Room drool over her, but that's not what I'm concerned about."

"Then what's bothering you?"

Pinchole looked around nervously, checking to make sure no one was in earshot. "Can we trust her?"

"What do you mean, can we *trust* her? You're the one who hired her!"

"I employ her as a highly qualified and competent computer analyst. We've only met with her twice, and she knows almost all of our operation. Even some of my right-hand men don't know as much as that girl."

The Doctor threw back his head and howled with laughter. "Do you think she's some kind of spy, an undercover agent out to destroy our operation? The girl is all of five feet and a hundred pounds. Unless those piercings are secret recording devices and her tattoos spout poison, I don't think we have anything to worry about."

"Pardon me for being paranoid. It's just that we're so close to getting the operation up and running. I don't want anything throwing a wrench in the works."

"The only person throwing a wrench is me. And I'm going to aim it right at your head if you bother me with this silliness again. Understand?"

Pinchole nodded.

"Good. Now, you had better get used to Stiv. I've decided she will be the newest member of my team. Our men are close to finding Daisha, correct?"

"They're scouring Palo Alto as we speak," Pinchole answered.

The Doctor's cell phone rang. He looked to see who was calling and then waved Pinchole away. "It's the governor of California. I have to take this call. Meet me back in my office in a couple hours to go over the final preparations."

The Doctor swallowed two prescription pain pills, hopped into an awaiting Bentley, and ordered his chauffeur back to his headquarters.

Chapter Thirty-Three

AXEL

Axel couldn't believe he was back at the Doctor's headquarters, standing beneath the same ventilation shaft where he had made his escape just the day before. All of his senses were on high alert. The four-mile walk from the center of Palo Alto had taken him over an hour. He was hot, sweaty, and dying for a drink of water.

Googleplex next door had provided the perfect cover as Axel had approached. The headquarters of the world's most popular search engine company was not only a bustling place to work, but also a tourist attraction. Dozens of people wandered the grounds, taking pictures of the public art and wacky Android lawn statues shaped like ice cream sandwiches, lollipops, doughnuts, and honeycombs. Axel nonchalantly fell in with a tour group. When they moved near the tree line that separated Googleplex from the Doctor's property, he rushed into the trees and made his way to the deserted loading dock in the back.

The metal grille that he had kicked out of the ventilation shaft was still lying on the asphalt. He figured that crawling back through the ductwork and dropping into the room was his best bet. But how could he get up there? The opening to the vent was a good ten feet up. He looked around for something to use as a ladder. The only thing close was a length of PVC pipe leaning against a Dumpster.

"It's long enough," Axel mused, leaning the pipe against the concrete wall. "But I'm going to have to channel my inner monkey to scurry up this baby."

After several failed attempts, he discovered the best way to shimmy up the pipe was upside down. He had made it halfway to the top when he saw a tractor-trailer truck driving up the road. The truck passed through the security gates and rolled toward the loading dock. Axel climbed faster, hand over hand, ankles crisscrossed around the pipe to hold him up. The entrance to the shaft was just above his head. If he were upright, crawling into the opening would be easy. But he was upside down, hanging precariously from the pipe.

Squealing truck brakes sent a chill up Axel's spine. He watched the driver position the truck and slowly back into the loading dock. The truck's backup warning beeps echoed off the building's walls. Before the driver noticed his presence, Axel contorted his body in midair and grabbed the lip of the ventilation shaft with his fingertips. The PVC pipe crashed to the ground. With a giant, white-knuckle heave, Axel pulled up his body weight and quickly hurried into the hole.

Darkness and dust enveloped him once again. After ten minutes of crawling, he dropped through the same ceiling he had used for his escape. Everything looked the same as he had left it. The security camera lay in pieces on the floor, and the food platter Pinchole had brought him was still sitting on a side table. Figuring the chicken skewers and cocktail wieners soaked in barbeque sauce were bad by now, he tore into the vegetable plate, gobbling down handfuls of broccoli, sweet peppers, cherry tomatoes, and celery. He thought of Daisha's empty belly and hoped that she was sitting down to a hot dinner of lentil curry and rice.

"From what I understand, we're all going," a deep voice bellowed from the hallway outside.

"I hate Indian food," said another voice. "That crap tastes and looks like dog puke. They got McDonald's over there?"

"McDonald's is everywhere."

Axel's heart fell through his stomach. He dove behind the couch just as two Pursuers entered the room.

"Throw that rotting food away," the first voice ordered.

"What about all of this broken surveillance equipment?" the other voice asked.

"Dump it and let's get out of here. Pinchole just texted from the airport. The cargo plane's loaded and ready to go. He'll be back here in an hour and wants a security detail in the Monitoring Room."

Axel heard the door slam and the men's footsteps fade away down the hall. He crawled from behind the couch. The presence of the men made him realize how difficult it would be to snatch back the GeoPort.

He slowly opened the door and peeked into the hallway. It was empty.

He spotted a closet next to the elevator. Axel rushed to the closet and threw open the door. There was nothing but cleaning supplies. Trash-can liners, floor cleaners, dozens of toilet paper rolls, refill jars of hand soap, two vacuum cleaners, a plastic towel dispenser with a broken handle, and a big yellow mop bucket and wringer on wheels. The overwhelming odor of disinfectant made his sinuses burn.

A shirt and baseball cap hanging on a hook caught

his attention. It was a janitor's uniform. The shirt was a light blue, long-sleeved button-down with green stripes. Two patches adorned the chest. One said *Manny*; the other said *Los Altos Janitorial Services*. The hat was green with the same Los Altos Janitorial Services logo. Inside the front shirt pocket was a blue handkerchief and single key attached to a San Francisco Giants key ring. A white sticky tag dangling from the metal loop said *Master*. Axel pulled on the shirt, buttoned it up, and tucked it into his jeans. The shirt was too big, but not by much. The hat fit perfectly, even with his long hair tucked underneath.

"The only way I'm getting into the Monitoring Room is as a janitor," he said to himself. "And I bet this master key will unlock the door. I can walk right inside without anyone suspecting a thing."

Axel pushed the mop bucket and wringer into the elevator and pressed the third floor button. A moment later, the doors shut and he was climbing toward the Monitoring Room.

Chapter Thirty-Four

DAISHA

Daisha was a streaming flood of supercharged electrical particles. She hurtled through the Warp at the speed of light, while flickering pictures like in a nineteenth-century kinetoscope flashed on the Warp's artery walls. Mostly the historic images were innocuous—ancient Ohlone people fishing in Adobe Creek and early settlers pushing plows. A few were more disturbing, like Franciscan missionaries enslaving, whipping, and even branding the local indigenous population.

When Axel was with her in the Warp, she always felt his warm, loving, and protective energy surging directly beside her. Those comforting feelings were not accompanying her this time, though, and she spewed from the Warp and hit the ground with a jaw-clenching crunch.

Daisha's head was spinning, and her stomach felt

sick. She took several long breaths before she took a look around. She quickly realized she was sprawled on top of a large oak desk. Strewn everywhere were papers, pens, photos, and other desktop knickknacks. She sat up and looked at a photo inside a cracked frame. The picture was of a very familiar-looking man shaking the hand of what looked like the president of the United States.

"Holy shitake mushroom!" she blurted out. "I've Warped right inside the Doctor's private office!"

Instantly, Daisha regretted her decision not to Warp directly to India as she had promised Axel. Her stomach knotted up. She had made a horrible mistake. By not going to India, she would have to wait a whole day until the Warp reset. And worst of all, she was now stuck inside the belly of the beast.

"How could I be so stupid?" she cried.

The Doctor's office door flew open. Daisha nearly leaped out of her skin. A young woman with shoulder-length platinum-blond hair stared at her from the doorway.

"Who are...What in the..." the woman stuttered, her eyes bugging out in shock. She plucked a cell phone from her pocket, but before the woman could hit a button, Daisha leaped to her feet, knocked the phone away, and tackled the woman to the carpet. The woman screamed and squirmed, trying to get free. But it was no use. Although Daisha was only thirteen, she was taller than the woman by a good four inches and had grown incredibly strong from dodging Pursuers.

"I'm not going to hurt you," Daisha said, trying to calm her down. She then heaved the woman to her feet and pushed her into a closet. After securing the back of a chair against the door handle to lock the woman inside, Daisha stepped into the lobby.

"I have to find a way out of here," Daisha murmured. "That woman will kick her way out of the closet in no time."

The Doctor's reception area was just as opulent as his office. Beautifully carved woodwork decorated the walls. Fancy leather couches and chairs surrounded a fireplace. A large elevator door painted to look like an Egyptian pharaoh's tomb dominated one wall. A fire escape door with a bright red sign above it that flashed Exit was adjacent to the elevator.

"Axel said the Monitoring Room was on the third floor," Daisha said to herself. "If we're going to hook up again, that's where I have to go."

She was about to push the elevator button but thought she would be safer taking the fire exit instead.

She burst through the door and hesitated for a moment, not knowing where to go. Then, seeing there were no stairs leading up, she bounded down the metal steps. A smile spread across her face when she reached a heavy steel door with a sign that read Third Floor, where Axel had said the Doctor was keeping the GeoPort.

The door was windowless, so Daisha couldn't see what was waiting on the other side. She pressed her ear against the door, listening for any sounds. Her palms were sweaty, her heart ricocheting. She knew all too well that just because she couldn't *hear* anybody on the other side of the door didn't mean no one was there waiting for her.

"Okay," Daisha said, trying to pump herself up. "If I didn't hear anything, then I guess it's safe." She took a deep breath, grabbed the handle, and peeked through the doorway. What was waiting for her on the other side caused her insides to swell with relief.

A short, skinny janitor in a baseball cap and a long-sleeved work shirt a size too big had stopped pushing a bucket and mop to stare at her. The janitor looked just as surprised as she was.

"Axel!" Daisha shouted.

"Hush up," Axel said, pressing a finger to his lips. "What are you doing here? You're supposed to be waiting for me in India."

"I was about to go, but I couldn't leave without you."

"How'd you sneak in here? I had to crawl through a ventilation shaft."

Daisha held up her GeoPort. "One time when I was bored in Vietnam, I googled the coordinates for the Doctor's headquarters. The latitude and longitude numbers stuck..."

The sound of an elevator opening and two loud voices talking cut her off in mid-sentence. "It's the Doctor!" Daisha exclaimed.

"The other guy is Pinchole, the head science geek. I'd recognize his wimpy voice anywhere."

"What do we do now?"

"I bet they're headed to the Monitoring Room. Quick, let's go back where you came from and figure out our next move."

Daisha and Axel hustled into the stairwell, the door slamming shut just as the Doctor, Pinchole, and four armed security guards rounded the corner.

Chapter Thirty-Five

DOCTOR STAIN

"Ouch!" the Doctor hollered as his foot collided with a big yellow bucket. "What's this thing doing in the middle of the hallway?"

Pinchole shrugged. "Don't know. One of the custodians must have left it."

"Remind me to tell Kari to fire these people and hire a new janitorial service."

One of the guards moved the bucket against the wall and joined the others stopped in front of the Monitoring Room. The room's security was state of the art. First, Pinchole punched a series of numbers on a pad on the wall. He then pressed his thumb against another pad for fingerprint recognition. Finally, he looked directly into a small camera lens embedded into the wall. Only when the system recognized his iris did the door pop open and allowed them to enter.

A dozen scientists, both male and female, scurried around the Monitoring Room. They operated dozens of laptop computers, antenna systems, communications modulators, signal conversion systems, subcarrier synthesizers, and a dozen other pieces of high-tech equipment. The two giant high-resolution monitors that once tracked Axel and Daisha via sophisticated reconnaissance satellites were now black.

"Unfortunately, we can't transport any of the Satellite Warp equipment to India," Pinchole explained. "I've handpicked these twelve individuals to man the ship while we're on location."

"Show me the GeoPort," the Doctor demanded.

Pinchole pulled a key from his pocket and walked over to a closet safe marked *Authorized Personnel Only*. He was just about to unlock the door when a young woman with blue hair, piercings, and colorful tattoos looked up from a laptop screen.

"What are you doing here?" Pinchole snarled.

"Working," Stiv said.

"The Doctor told you to go home and pack, not to come back to the Monitoring Room."

"I needed to get some things together so I could be of better assistance in India."

"Well, I don't think..."

"Stop it right there," the Doctor ordered. "The girl is part of my team. She doesn't need the third degree from you. Now, get me the GeoPort."

"Yes, sir," Pinchole sighed and unlocked the safe. He stepped inside and emerged a moment later with the prize.

"The thing looks like a cheap cell phone," the Doctor said, taking the GeoPort from Pinchole.

"It's far from cheap. That little unit you're holding is worth more than all the proverbial tea in China."

The Doctor laughed. "Try worth more than all the bars of gold in Fort Knox and then some. I want you to fill me in on how this unit and a very expensive expedition to India are going to get the Doctor Lennon Hatch Geographical Transportation Company a New York Stock Exchange ticker symbol."

Stiv stood up from her desk. "May I see the GeoPort?"

"Of course, young lady," the Doctor said, handing her the unit.

"This isn't show-and-tell!" Pinchole whined. "I'm not comfortable passing around the world's greatest technological achievement like a toy truck."

"Quiet, you," the Doctor said sharply. "Once again, I want you to fill me in on what we hope to accomplish in India. Layman's terms, please."

Still obviously miffed at Stiv's presence, Pinchole clarified the entire operation as simply as possible. He explained that the realization that Magnes Solis was a place instead of a person was the key to unlocking the mystery. Further investigation into the Konanavlah Sun Temple's hyperactive magnetic properties had convinced him that the location was in fact a permanent electron diffusion region, or X-Point.

"I know all of that," the Doctor grumbled. "But how are you going to use that information to make our own GeoPort? From what you've told me, the two GeoPorts in existence won't work unless they are in very close proximity to each other."

"We already know that geographical transportation works using large space magnets to capture electrons found in the solar wind," Pinchole continued. "Then we transfer the electrons to Earth with lasers. This is enough power to dematerialize the human body. However, to make an actual working GeoPort, we needed to find a permanent, uninterrupted X-Point that connects the magnetic fields of the sun and Earth. The Konanavlah Sun Temple is that place. The GeoPort needs the power of a continuous portal to operate. Before now, we only knew how to follow the GeoPort's trail with limited success. Understand?"

"I understand perfectly," Stiv said, her eyes wide with wonder. "It's the same barrage of supercharged electrical particles that brighten the aurora borealis and ignite geomagnetic storms."

"Exactly. Thanks to Professors Jack and Tandala, we now know how to harness this incredible power. The world will never be the same again."

The Doctor smirked. "That is the understatement of the twenty-first century. You still haven't told me how you are going to corral this energy from the other side of the world."

Pinchole smiled. "Very carefully."

"Oh crap!" A voice rang out.

They looked up and saw that one of the Satellite Warp technicians had spilled a large bottle of fizzy, super-gulp cola all over the desk and floor.

"Get that mess cleaned up right away," Pinchole ordered. "Sugar water and electronic equipment don't mix."

The SWT grabbed a handful of napkins to sop up the spillage.

"There's a mop and bucket with a wringer outside in the hallway," the Doctor told one of his security guards. "Go out and get it."

The Doctor's cell phone rang. "Doctor Lennon

Hatch," he said. "Whoa...slow down, Kari. What is the matter? Why are you crying?"

Pinchole, taking advantage of the Doctor's diverted attention, snatched the GeoPort out of Stiv's hand. "This will remain under lock and key from now on, and no one touches it but me," he growled.

"Are you absolutely one-hundred-percent sure?" the Doctor asked, still talking into the phone. "I don't know whether to jump for joy or scream bloody murder. Alert security right away, please."

"What's going on?" Pinchole asked.

The Doctor hung up the call and slipped the phone back into his pocket. "That was Kari. A few moments ago, a young black girl with short hair attacked her in my office."

"What does this mean?" Stiv wondered.

"It means that Daisha Tandala has somehow sneaked into the building," the Doctor said, adjusting his arm sling. "She's here right now."

Chapter Thirty-Six

AXEL

Axel had just stepped into the hallway again when a Pursuer confronted him.

"Are you the janitor?" the guard asked.

"Uh-huh," Axel muttered, pulling his hat farther over his eyes and deepening his voice to sound older.

"Grab that mop and bucket. There's a mess in here to clean up."

Three more burly Pursuers burst out of the Monitoring Room and rushed down the hallway. Axel prayed they wouldn't head into the fire escape where Daisha was hiding. Much to his relief, they flew past the exit door and jumped into the elevator. The Pursuer who had ordered him to clean up joined them. The elevator doors closed and they were gone.

The argument Axel had had with Daisha just moments before replayed in his mind. He felt bad for scolding her, but using her GeoPort to Warp to the Doctor's headquarters instead of India was probably the stupidest thing in the world. Twenty-four hours had to pass before her GeoPort could work again. He hoped that she had taken his advice and was now crawling through the same ductwork he had used for escape. That way she could hide out for a day until the Warp was ready to go.

Regardless, he had to get his GeoPort back. The mop, bucket, and janitor disguise were his ticket into the Monitoring Room.

With a thumping heart and sweaty palms, he cautiously entered the room, leaving the door slightly ajar in case there was some kind of security lockdown mechanism. A young bearded man wearing a T-shirt with a picture of a fried egg and the words *This is your brain on HTML* pointed toward a large puddle of spilled soda. Axel kept his head down as he walked past the Doctor and Pinchole. He quickly took out the mop and began swabbing away. He listened intently to the heated conversation between the Doctor, Pinchole, and a girl with spiky blue hair and a gold hoop protruding from her bottom lip.

"If they're still in the building, the men will catch them," he heard Pinchole say.

"But why in the world would they come back?" the Doctor asked.

"That thing," Stiv said, snatching a small device from Pinchole's hands.

Axel's thoughts screamed silently inside his head—My GeoPort!

Pinchole grabbed the GeoPort back. "We still don't know how to replicate this precious device, and we need it. When we get to India, we'll start manipulating the Sun Temple's permanent X-Point. My team will advance the discoveries made by Professors Jack and Tandala by light-years."

"How exactly will you manipulate the X-Point?" Stiv asked.

"The same way you get to Carnegie Hall," Pinchole answered. "Practice, practice, practice!"

Stiv cocked her head and smirked. "Come on. Seriously."

"I am serious. Practice makes perfect, and I've been practicing with the Warp for over a year by sending men chasing down this little nugget." He held up the GeoPort and pretended to give it a kiss. "Since we have only one, it's impossible to use it like the kids did because of its security features. But all that changed when the girl steered us toward the discovery of a permanent

X-Point and its unfathomable power. And when I applied the simplicity of Faraday's Law to what we already knew, the whole shebang made perfect sense."

"Faraday what?" the Doctor asked.

"Faraday was a nineteenth-century English physicist who discovered that when a magnetic field changes, you create an electric current," Stiv offered. "It's eighth-grade science."

"Exactly," Pinchole interjected. "Faraday discovered that the bigger the changes in the magnetic field, the greater the amounts of voltage. A permanent X-Point is the Big Bang of earthly magnetic fields. If that field shifted or suddenly became demagnetized somehow, geographical transportation could not exist, unless we could find another X-Point."

As Axel eavesdropped, the realization hit him like a wet mop right in the face. His father and Daisha's mother didn't mean for them to destroy the GeoPorts; they meant for them to demagnetize the X-Point!

"I'm going to put this GeoPort back under lock and key until we're ready to jet to India," Pinchole said and made a step toward the closet safe.

The Monitoring Room door flew open. Daisha burst into the room, her eyes wild with adrenaline.

"Axel, get the GeoPort!" she screamed.

The Doctor gasped. "It's Daisha! And that janitor is Axel! Stop them!"

Axel took advantage of the diversion and leaped into action. He swung his mop handle like a baseball bat, clipping Pinchole in the ribs. The man grunted in pain as the GeoPort flew from his hands and skittered across the floor. Axel shoved one of the Satellite Warp techs aside and scooped up the GeoPort. He then tore out of the Monitoring Room with Daisha by his side. He didn't get ten yards before a Pursuer rounded a corner. The man clubbed him in the back of the head and grabbed him by the throat. Axel's eyes bugged out, his windpipe crushing under the Pursuer's viselike grip. He gasped for breath, clawing at the hand around his throat.

The Pursuer pulled out a gun and held it to Axel's temple.

"You better not move a muscle!" the Pursuer screamed, his spittle flying everywhere.

Out of the corner of his eye, Axel saw Daisha lunge at the Pursuer. She grabbed the arm attached to the hand around Axel's neck and bit hard into his flesh. The Pursuer cried out, aimed the gun at her, and fired. The blast was deafening. Axel's ears rang. When the smoke cleared, Axel saw a large bullet hole in the wall.

The shot had completely missed Daisha.

"Do not damage that GeoPort!" he heard Pinchole cry from down the hall.

Daisha kicked the Pursuer hard in the groin. The gun fell from his hand, and he crumpled to the floor.

The Doctor, Pinchole, and the girl with blue hair were closing in on them fast. Axel climbed to his feet, and he and Daisha took off down the hall. The elevator door opened, and the four burly Pursuers he had seen earlier sprinted in his direction with guns drawn.

"Hurry!" Daisha cried. "Type in the Sun Temple coordinates!"

Quickly Axel typed 23.1483° N, 79.9015° E, his fingers shaking.

"What about you?" Axel asked, out of breath.

As the Doctor, Pinchole, and the four Pursuers were about to pounce, Daisha pressed her thumb on the GeoPort's DNA sensor. Axel positioned his thumb next to hers and pushed the button.

Milliseconds later, both of them detonated into the invisible void.

Chapter Thirty-Seven

DAISHA

Daisha landed hard on a blistering hot, dusty dirt road. Her stomach heaved and her head throbbed from the blast through the Warp. After the cobwebs cleared, she looked for Axel. He was a few feet from her, on his hands and knees, vomiting.

"Sorry," he choked. "It's been a couple months since I've blown chunks after going through the Warp."

"Trust me," Daisha said. "If I had any food in my stomach, I'd be tossing cookies right beside you."

Axel wiped his mouth and sat back on his haunches. "I guess our parents didn't live long enough to fill us in on that little detail," he said.

"What detail?"

"When we pressed our thumbs together on the button, it must have recognized both of our DNA, allowing us to soar through the Warp with a single GeoPort."

"Maybe it was another safety feature our parents programmed into the unit," she said. "They made them both operable with either of our DNA. You know, in case we lost one or something."

Three women wearing beautiful saris and carrying large woven baskets filled with food shuffled past them. The mouthwatering smell of the exotic spices made Daisha's stomach grumble with hunger. Right behind the women came a long line of Japanese tourists. Expensive-looking cameras dangled around their necks, and all of them wore the same bright-yellow baseball caps. Daisha sat up and turned her head in the direction everyone was walking. There, bathed in golden rays of morning sunshine, stood the monument she and Axel had been running toward for six months without even knowing it.

The Konanavlah Sun Temple.

The ruins of the majestic structure stood before her like seven prancing horses pulling a giant chariot. Daisha knew from her Internet search that the shrine was supposed to represent that. She remembered that the temple was from the tenth century and that some ancient king had built it to honor the Hindu Sun God, Surya.

"Wow," Axel said with wonderment. "That thing is

just freaking wow. Look at those intricately carved walls and pillars. Whoever built this baby was an artistic genius."

"See those three huge, entwined elephant tusks?" Daisha pointed out. "I read that the ancient architects always used that symbol as their trademark."

"They must have really liked fighting elephants too, because the imagery is everywhere."

The amazement of gazing at the Sun Temple up close and personal quickly gave way to paranoia. A bead of anxious sweat rolled down Daisha's temple as her eyes darted back and forth, looking for the Doctor's men.

"I don't see any Pursuers," she said. "At least I don't see them yet."

"What should we do now?" Axel asked.

Daisha let out a nervous chuckle. "Well, *Manny*. You can start by ditching the janitor's uniform, unless you want to do free advertising for Los Altos Janitorial Services."

Axel stuck his tongue out at her. "My other shirt has a big rip in it. I'm fine with this one."

Daisha pointed to a blue handkerchief lying in the dirt. "Is that yours?" she asked.

"Yes. I found it in the chest pocket of the work shirt. It must've fallen out when I landed."

"Did you blow your nose with it?"

"No. I just used it to wipe some sweat off my forehead back at the Doctor's building."

"Then I'm keeping it," Daisha said, snatching the hankie off the ground and shoving it in her front pocket. "I might need it for something down the road."

"The tour is about to start!" a man with a thick Indian accent shouted.

The Japanese visitors joined a handful of British couples.

"There's safety in numbers," Daisha said. "Let's disappear in the tour group. Maybe we can figure out what our parents want us to do here."

"I already know what they want us to do," Axel said.

"What?"

"Thanks to that virus, Pinchole, I figured out they didn't mean for us to destroy the GeoPorts," Axel said. "They want us to demagnetize the X-Point. Because of our parents' discovery, the Konanavlah Sun Temple is the only known X-Point in the world. Without its intense magnetism, the Doctor can't go through with his plans."

Daisha stood silent for a long moment, digesting what Axel had told her. "So you're saying the X-Point makes the GeoPort work. Without the X-Point, no

Doctor Lennon Hatch Geographical Transportation Company or whatever he wants to call his stupid business."

"Exactly."

"How do you propose we destroy one of the most invincible natural forces in our solar system?"

Axel shrugged. "Maybe this tour guide will let us know."

They listened as the tour guide explained the temple's ancient Brahman origins. The tour then entered a doorway guarded by statues of two huge war elephants.

"We are now in the Gathering Hall," the guide explained. "This was an area of sacred dancing in honor of Surya, the Sun God."

Axel whispered in Daisha's ear. "Maybe Surya will help us destroy this X-Point."

"Shhhh," Daisha hushed, pressing a finger to her lips. "I want to hear everything he has to say."

An unfathomable collage of intricate, ornate stone carvings covered every inch of the temple. To Daisha, the whole thing felt like a massive, 3-D Magic Eye illusion. She squinted her eyes, staring in one place and expecting a hidden picture to reveal itself.

The guide continued. "The temple entrance was carefully positioned to capture the first rays of the sun. The temple and its team of horses face east to pull the chariot toward the rising sun. The seven carved horses represent the days of the week, and the temple has twelve balconies to represent the months of the year."

As the tour moved toward the north end of the temple, a tall, handsome Indian man with a thick, black mustache and wearing a long, white dhoti approached them.

"The temple is beautiful even in its ruins," the man commented.

"Extremely," Daisha said.

"Pretty awesome," Axel added.

The man pointed to an exquisite carving of a half-bird, half-man creature sitting on the back of an elephant that appeared to be fighting a giant cobra. "That ancient deity is Garuda," the man said. "Traditionally, Garuda has the golden body of a muscular man, powerful red wings, a white face, and the sharp beak of an eagle. He also wears a crown on his head. A modern-day sea eagle called the Brahminy kite is a living representation of Garuda. In fact, I saw a breeding pair fly over the temple moments ago."

"What kind of god is this Garuda?" Axel asked.

"Garuda is the king of all birds and the enemy of snakes. He represents freedom from tyranny and the promise of courage at the time of catastrophe. He is also the idol that carries Lord Vishnu, the Protector of the World."

"What does Vishnu protect the world from?" Daisha wondered.

"Vishnu is the divine being of peace, compassion, and mercy. Anything that tries to upset that balance is the Lord's enemy."

He smiled. "My name is Jagannath. My Western friends call me Jag. What are your names?"

"Ax—" Axel blurted out but then stopped himself.

"Nice to meet you, Ax." Jag turned to Daisha. "And you are?"

"Danielle," Daisha said, remembering the phony name she had given the police officer back in Ohio.

"Ax and Danielle. I can tell from your accents you must be from the United States or perhaps Canada."

Daisha and Axel gave each other a suspicious glance, indicating that Jag was getting a little too nosy and it was time to rejoin the tour group.

As they attempted to move on, Jag blocked their way with his large frame. "The temple is also said to be one of the most magnetic places on Earth," he said, his black eyes glistening with intensity. "Legend has it that powerful magnets placed in the temple's tower allowed the king's throne to float in midair."

"Thanks for sharing, but we have to get back to the group," Daisha said quickly.

Jag reached out and pressed his palm against the carving of Garuda. The deity's image creaked open like the door to a crypt. Before Daisha and Axel could react, Jag shoved them into the opening and then quickly closed the door.

Darkness enveloped them. Daisha's heart rushed with panic. She pounded on the hard stone walls, screaming for Jag to let them out. The *whoosh* sound of a fire igniting filled her ears. Bright orange-yellow light filled the chamber. Sweet-smelling incense wafted in the air. Flower garlands, colorful fabrics, and strings of bells decorated one wall. Hanging on another wall was a massive tapestry picturing the unmistakable likeness of Garuda. Perched on top of the king of birds was Vishnu. The god had skin the color of a cloudless summer sky, four arms, and a crown of jewels on his head.

Daisha looked around and saw two fiery torches about eight feet apart. Sitting between the torches was an old Indian man with a long, white beard and equally long, white hair. He was almost naked except for a blue cloth covering from his waist down. With eyes closed, the yogi levitated a foot off the ground in a lotus position.

“Who are you?” Daisha cried out.

The man’s eyes snapped open. He stared at them, the expression on his face full of bliss and complete serenity.

“Welcome,” he said with a strong yet calm voice. “We’ve been waiting for you.”

Chapter Thirty-Eight
DOCTOR STAIN

The Doctor's private jet landed on time at the Jabalpur Airport. From there, he, Pinchole, and Stiv hopped into a chauffeured van and headed to a meeting with the governor of Madhya Pradesh and his chief minister. Also scheduled to attend were the director of tourism and a professor from the Jabalpur Engineering College.

Motorcycles, bicycles, buses, and pedestrians clogged the claustrophobic streets. The van's horn blared as the driver weaved in and around the masses of humanity. The Doctor rolled down his window and watched the street life. A blast of hot, humid air made the port-wine stain on his face throb. He had never been to India before, and the frenetic energy made him slightly dizzy. Adolescent boys pulled huge carts of rice, numerous food stands sold fruit and vegetables, and women balanced boxes on their heads while walking at the same time. The sounds of loud car engines and people shouting, hooting, and hollering rang inside his ears. He quickly rolled the window back up when a truck with choking exhaust billowing from its tailpipe pulled up beside them.

"I just got a text from one of my SW techs," Pinchole said, staring at his phone. "The cargo plane has landed and been unloaded, and everything is en route to the temple."

"Excellent," the Doctor said. "Please explain what we need to tell these officials at our meeting. Of course, any objections to our project will be answered with personal checks containing a lot of zeroes at the end."

"Make sure you make one of those checks out to me," Pinchole joked.

The Doctor dug a pen under the cast on his wrist, trying to alleviate an itch. "Young man, a good chunk of my money is already going to you."

"What you will tell the Indian officials and the true nature of our mission are two very different things," Pinchole explained. "As far as the Indians are concerned, we are in their country to study the magnetic properties of the Sun Temple to generate power—as in electricity. We'll explain that our aim is to create a new form of clean energy from Earth's magnetic field and the solar wind." He reached into his briefcase and pulled out a laptop. "To convince the representative from the engineering college, I've created a PowerPoint presentation. Don't worry. I'll do most of the talking. You can save your energy for shaking hands, posing for pictures, and greasing greedy fingers."

"They'll love the clean-energy mumbo jumbo," the Doctor said. "We'll make nuclear plants and coal obsolete, fresh air for everybody, no more global warming, yadda, yadda, yadda."

"But what are you really going to do here?" Stiv asked. "That's what I'm dying to hear about."

Pinchole scowled at her. The Doctor chuckled. He knew that Stiv's sudden inclusion in the inner circle annoyed his director of Satellite Warp science to no end. To Pinchole, the girl was a splinter under his nail. A spiky-haired, tattooed Yoko Ono breaking up his math and physics version of the Beatles.

"Tell her," the Doctor said. "I'd like to get up to speed myself too."

"What Professors Jack and Tandala did here was small scale compared to what we are going to do," Pinchole explained. "They only manipulated the magnetic properties enough to create two working GeoPorts. I've deduced this was because they didn't want to damage the temple. However, to accomplish our goals, we must destroy the structure completely."

"But you can't destroy it," Stiv argued. "The Konanavlah Sun Temple is a thousand-year-old Hindu shrine."

"As I was saying," Pinchole continued, completely ignoring Stiv's objections. "The esteemed professors only manipulated the magnetic properties a very small amount. To make a worldwide geographical transportation system, we will rev this baby into overdrive."

"How will you do that?" the Doctor asked. "I want to know exactly what my money is helping you accomplish."

"The solar wind erupts from the sun in a blast of ion cyclotron and magnetohydrodynamic waves. They hurtle toward Earth at a million miles per hour. It's one of the most powerful and fascinating phenomena in the solar system. The only thing that saves us from destruction is our magnetized atmosphere. We use space magnets to capture those waves and then transfer them to Earth with lasers. Until we knew about the permanent X-Point, we sent those watered-down waves to satellites on the roof of the Doctor's building. Now we will harness its full power, sending it directly to the temple. Our men and equipment will do the work from there."

"A one-thousand-year-old collection of carved stone can't withstand that type of solar onslaught," Stiv remarked, a hint of sadness in her voice.

"A horrible, unfortunate accident," the Doctor said, pretending to speak before news reporters. "This loss of antiquity cannot be replaced, but I will make restitution to the Indian government and make sure that a tragedy like this never happens again."

"You're good," Stiv commented.

"I'm the best," he said with a wink.

Pinchole stifled an air pollution–induced sneeze. "The temple's sacrifice will give us the greatest power the world has ever known, the ability to dematerialize the elemental composition of the human body to a stream of charged particles, and then reconstitute those particles back to human form."

"With the added bonus of transferring a person to any latitudinal and longitudinal point on Earth and making me the most powerful human being who ever walked on two legs," the Doctor said.

The van screeched to a stop in front of a large government building.

"This must be the place," Pinchole said, putting away his laptop and zipping his bags.

"Stiv, you stay here in the van," the Doctor instructed.

"I may go wander around the shops for a while," Stiv said.

"Fine, but don't go far." The Doctor dug into his pocket, pulled out a wad of rupees, and handed half to Stiv and the other half to the driver. "Be careful. I wouldn't want anything to happen to the newest member on my team."

The Doctor and Pinchole hopped out of the car and bounded up a long set of marble steps. Just as the Doctor was about to open the building's lavish rosewood doors, the urge to look back at Stiv overwhelmed him. He turned his head and watched her run across the road, dodging cars and motorcycles, disappearing into the crowd.

Chapter Thirty-Nine

AXEL

The old Indian man who had been defying gravity slowly drifted back to solid ground. He rested on a mound of pillows, his dark eyes wise and penetrating. Axel was about to ask him where they were when Jag appeared from the shadows. He was carrying a platter of mouthwatering food.

"Forgive me if I frightened you," Jag said, setting the platter on a marble table. "But it was the only way to get you into the library. Please eat. You must be very hungry after such a long trip."

Axel and Daisha tore into the food. They piled their plates high with jasmine rice, spinach paneer, and chickpea masala, sopping everything up with hot garlic naan.

"This is the strangest library I've ever been inside," Daisha said through a mouthful of rice.

"Who are you?" Axel demanded as he bit into his third piece of naan.

"I already told you my name," Jag answered, and then pointed to the man sitting on the pillows. "His name is Larraj, the most gifted Nadi reader in all of India."

"A Nadi what?" Axel questioned.

Larraj cleared his throat. "Nadi means *in search of* in the Tamil language," he said with a thick Indian accent. "I am the keeper and interpreter of the ancient writings. You are standing within the walls of the Konanavlah Palm Leaf Library."

"I don't understand," Daisha said. "What's a palm leaf library?"

"Before you ask any more questions, I must take your fingerprints so Larraj can identify your set of palm leaves," Jag said. "Axel, because you are male, the print must come from your right thumb. Daisha, as a female, yours must come from the left thumb."

"How do you know our real names?" Axel asked. "I've never met you in my life."

"All of your questions will be answered shortly," Jag said and produced two pieces of black card stock. He gripped Axel's thumb and pressed it firmly against the paper. When he had Daisha's print, he handed both to Larraj. The Nadi reader carefully studied the prints, stood up, and walked to the far end of the room. Because of the dim firelight, Axel hadn't realized that all around them were rows of wooden shelves, each containing stacks of bundled palm leaves.

"I have a fingerprint match," Larraj said, smiling. "Of course, this was just a mere formality as I have been studying these particular leaves for most of my life. The seven sages—Atri, Bhrigu, Angira, Gautama, Kashyapa, Agastya, and Vashishta—wrote them out of compassion for all of humanity. Thousands of years ago they predicted the exact date and time for when both the dark and bright sides of the moon would manifest in human form."

"When I laid eyes on you in the courtyard," Jag said. "I knew without a doubt you two were the dark and bright sides of the moon the prophecy had foretold."

Larraj held up a bundle of dried palm leaves tied together with string and covered with squiggly lines. "The seven sages were living at such high levels of consciousness that they could see through time and space," he explained. "Because of this ability, they were able to peer into the lives of people all around the world, including those not yet born. Every human who has lived or will ever live has their prophecy written on a palm leaf somewhere in this library."

"The uniqueness of your thumbprint identifies your individual palm leaf," Jag offered. "That is why I needed to take them."

"The palm leaves I hold in my hands contain the very first foretelling written by the seven sages," Larraj continued. "It is as old as our civilization itself. The premonition, which is written in Sanskrit, is divinely directed at both of you."

"Prove it," Axel said. "What do they say specifically that identifies Daisha and me?"

Larraj read from the first palm leaf. "Young man, it says here your name is Axel. You were born on April 19. Young lady, you are Daisha. Your date of birth is August 10.

"He's right!" Daisha cried.

"You are both only children and were born in a place called Palo Alto, California."

A chill went up Axel's spine. He reached out and grabbed Daisha's hand. Her skin was clammy, and he could tell that she was just as freaked out as he was.

"How could a dried-up leaf thousands of years old contain my name, birthday, and the place I was born?" Axel wondered.

Jag pressed a finger to his lips, indicating that there was a lot more to come.

"Your parents were great teachers and scientists. They worked together on the mysteries of the universe."

Daisha's mouth fell open in utter astonishment.

"A very powerful red shadow murdered them in a place meant for dogs. That shadow also wants to kill you two." Larraj turned to the next palm leaf. "From the expressions on your faces, I assume that you believe what I am saying. Correct?"

"Yes," Axel muttered. "I'm sold. This is creepy and fascinating at the same time."

"What I will read next does not begin at your birth, but from the moment when you will face the biggest challenge of your lives. Your moment of doubt and pain, so they say, is now. Shall we begin?"

"No...yes," Daisha stuttered. "I-I don't know!"

"Let's have it," Axel said. "Maybe it will let us know how to demagnetize this temple and save the world from the Doctor."

Jag and Larraj shot each other a knowing glance.

"Axel, I think you may be as prophetic as the seven sages," Larraj commented. "Are you two absolutely sure you want me to continue?"

Axel and Daisha nodded.

"On June 21 of this year on the summer solstice," Larraj read, "the moon will fall from the sky, landing at the Konanavlah Sun Temple. The bright side will be male, recognizable by his pale skin and long, curly hair the muddy color of the Narmada River. The dark side will be female, shadowy and beautiful like the goddess Parvati, wife of Shiva and mother of Ganesha. Garuda will fly overhead disguised as two sea eagles, indicating their arrival."

Axel and Daisha sat in stunned silence as Larraj continued the reading. They learned that the Sun Temple had been under assault almost since its creation—all because of its magnificent, awe-inspiring magnetic properties. Larraj also explained that the seven sages thought the dark and bright sides of the moon were the children of the gods. The first prophecy was devoted solely to them so they could gain wisdom and insight before their monumental undertaking.

"What is the undertaking?" Axel asked.

"You already know," Larraj said. "By demagnetizing the temple, you free its soul so the divine energy may return to Swarga, the place you call Heaven. You will also stop the temple's destruction and save the world from the shadow."

"My own Nadi palm leaf has destined me to help save the Sun Temple from destruction," Jag said. "That is why I am here with you now."

"I want to know how we're supposed to defeat this shadow," Daisha said.

Larraj pulled out a new palm leaf. This one was so faded that the squiggly lines of the scrawled Sanskrit were barely legible. "The leaf says that you must use the shadow's own power and destroy it from within," he said. "A small cloud will break away from the shadow's thunderstorm and assist you." Larraj stopped reading and stared at them for a long moment, his serene face growing long with concern. "As for the rest of the prophecy, I think our consultation should end here."

"It can't end!" Axel exclaimed. "I want those leaves to tell us how to defeat him!"

Daisha grabbed Axel's elbow. "Calm down," she hushed.

"Don't tell me to calm down," Axel said, tearing his arm from Daisha's grasp. "Jag throws us in here against our will, and some yoga dude gives us one colossal mind freak by reading our lives like a Wikipedia page. Tell us how to defeat him!"

Larraj looked down at the palm leaf and then back at Axel. "The final divination says that the boy with hair like the muddy Narmada River must die yet still live. Now, you must leave. The consultation is over."

Jag pressed his palm against a wall, and a door

opened onto an empty courtyard. He then shoved Axel and Daisha out of library and into the brilliant sunshine.

Chapter Forty

STIV

Stiv's heart pounded as she rushed through the busy streets of Jabalpur. Truck horns blared, motorcycle engines whined, pariah dogs yowled, and hordes of people shouted back and forth over the deafening traffic noise.

"Sorry," Stiv apologized after nearly plowing over an old man pushing a cart full of freshly baked naan bread.

The people, traffic, and shops stretched toward the horizon. Stiv hadn't planned to escape from the Doctor this early in the trip, but the moment had presented itself and she took advantage. Thankfully, the man had given her the stack of rupees. The cash would make getting to the Sun Temple all that more convenient.

"Young lady, you are British?" a female shopkeeper standing with dirty bare feet and wearing a bright-pink sari asked in broken English.

Stiv stopped running and peered into the shop. Rows of exotic Indian dresses and stacks of colorful, silky fabrics filled nearly every inch of the space. The sweet smell of jasmine incense wafted in the air, making a nice contrast to the stinky stench of the streets.

"I'm an American," Stiv answered back.

"Your clothing," the shopkeeper said. "They are like what a man wears. Come inside and try on proper dress."

A full-length mirror near the door confirmed the shopkeeper's fashion assessment. Stiv was wearing leather pants, black motorcycle boots, a ratty T-shirt, and a sleeveless jean jacket with the rock lyrics *I hate men who think I'm afraid* scrawled in black marker.

"Yes," Stiv said. "I would like to purchase new clothes."

The shopkeeper smiled and invited her into the shop.

"Do you have a washroom?" Stiv asked.

A confused look spread on the shopkeeper face, as if not understanding the meaning of the word *washroom*.

"Clean," Stiv said, and then mimed the act of scrubbing her face and arms.

"Ah, yes," the shopkeeper said. "Behind the curtain. In back."

Stiv had expected to find a toilet and sink behind the

curtain. Instead, she saw a wooden stool on which sat a chipped porcelain bowl filled with suspicious-looking gray water. A white towel and small mirror hung on a pair of wall hooks.

"At least the towel looks clean," she said to herself and splashed her face with water. Thick black mascara ran down her cheeks. After wiping the makeup from her face, she removed all of her lip and ear piercings—sixteen in all—and shoved them in her pocket.

Ridding herself of the tattoos came next. She dipped the towel in water and scrubbed her upper right arm. The complicated blend of lilacs, gardenias, and unicorns she had painstakingly drawn on herself to resemble permanent tattoos melted down her arm in a gush of rainbow colors. She ran a finger through her short, spiky blue hair. Nothing she could do about her head except cover it with a scarf. The long, black hair she had worn since elementary school would take a while to grow back.

She stared at her face in the mirror. Stiv and the punk persona she had created for herself were gone. Once again, she was Megan, a Stanford University PhD candidate in applied physics from Palo Alto, California.

The shopkeeper was waiting with a tape measure. "I will make a good fit. You will be beautiful."

With the proper measurements taken, Stiv browsed through rows of saris. They ranged from simple and modest to designer and glamorous. An embroidered aqua-blue sari with a matching headscarf caught her attention.

"It looks nice on you," the shopkeeper said, taking the sari off the rack.

After a brief tutorial on how to wear the traditional Indian dress, Stiv stepped behind the curtain. She slipped on the skirt and top and then wrapped herself in the long, silky fabric. The softness of the sari felt luxurious against her skin. After pinning everything together, she emerged from behind the curtain.

The shopkeeper wrapped the matching scarf around her head. "Lovely," she said. "You look like Indian princess."

Stiv counted out the money and handed the shopkeeper a stack of bills with Gandhi's picture. She was relieved that after paying for the dress, there was still a lot of money left from what the Doctor had originally given her.

"How do I get to the Konanavlah Sun Temple?" she asked.

"Temple seventy kilometers from here. You can take train from station, but it dangerous for woman to travel alone. You need a man."

I hate men who think I'm afraid.

The quote she had written on her jean jacket popped into her mind. There was only one man she hated—Doctor Lennon Hatch. After all, he was the one responsible for killing her mentors and all-time favorite people in the world—professors Roswell Jack and Jodiann Tandala.

Out of all the qualified candidates, the professors had made her their number one lab assistant. They trusted her enough to let only her in on the amazing secret of geographical transportation. Not for one second did she believe they cooked meth in their lab or that a Mexican drug cartel had killed them. After some serious sleuthing, she knew without a doubt that the Doctor had ordered their hit and exactly why he had killed them.

However, until the incident in the Monitoring Room with the kids, she was not sure that Axel and Daisha were still alive. Now she had seen them with her own eyes, Warping away in the hallway of the Doctor's headquarters. A deep intuitive feeling told her they were in India right now. Specifically, they were heading to the Konanavlah Sun Temple to save the world just like she was.

"How do I get to the train station?" Stiv asked.

"Walk north," the shopkeeper instructed. "Less than a kilometer from here." The shopkeeper tried to give back her old clothes. "Do you want these in sack?"

"No. I won't need them anymore."

Megan then dashed out of the shop, heading straight for the train station.

Chapter Forty-One

DOCTOR STAIN

Fourteen BharatBenz freight trucks sat idling on India Route 30 in front of the gated entrance of the Konanavlah Sun Temple. The trucks had rolled over miles of dusty roads pocked with potholes from the Jabalpur Airport, carrying all of the equipment needed to harness the solar wind and manipulate the X-Point.

"We shouldn't have left Stiv," the Doctor said, his voice filled with worry.

"There was no choice," Pinchole remarked. "The Indian officials only agreed to shut down the temple to visitors for three weeks. The platoon of soldiers they gave us for security goes away then too.

The Doctor chuckled. "That whole meeting was just for show. As long as I keep padding their bank accounts, we can keep this placed closed as long as we want."

"Yes. But we still have to get busy unloading

trucks, setting up the equipment, and"—adding air quotes—"*investigating new and viable sources of green energy*. The party must start with or without your latest crush."

The Doctor shot Pinchole an angry look. "Watch your mouth, and remember who you're speaking to."

"I'm sorry, but we couldn't suspend the operation until she turned up. After all, you told her not to wander far. Three of our men are pounding the streets of Jabalpur looking for her as we speak. I guarantee you they'll find her sitting in some shop getting a henna tattoo, blissfully unaware of the aggravation she has caused you."

"You're probably right. Let the festivities begin."

Pinchole signaled three guards from the Indian Armed Forces to open the gate. The line of trucks rolled into the Sun Temple's main compound. Pinchole waved the vehicles into position. He ordered four huge satellite dishes to go on the Sun Temple's north, west, south, and east corners. The 800 MHz nuclear magnetic resonance spectrometer was to be set up in the courtyard, and several powerful x-ray lasers would dot the exterior grounds.

"The magic is how we can make solar energy self-sustaining," Pinchole said over the clatter of the hydraulic forklifts. "Without our thermoelectric converters, Earth's atmosphere would just dissipate the energy before it reached our satellite dishes."

"What do we do with all this energy once we have it?" the Doctor asked.

Pinchole pointed toward two freight trucks. "See those trucks?"

"What about them?"

"Inside each trailer are massive lithium-ion batteries of 365–560 Wh/kgs. They're the same batteries that powered NASA's deep-space probes like *Voyager 2*, *New Horizons*, and *Juno*. They will store the energy until we start construction on an electromagnetic radiation power plant. Thanks to your recent land acquisitions, the plant will break ground less than two kilometers from here sometime in the next six months."

"Those batteries had to cost a pretty penny."

"Yes, about as much as the four long cables running from the satellites to the trucks."

The Doctor scratched his enflamed cheek. "They look like cheap garden hoses."

"They may look like a dollar-store deal, but in reality the hoses are made from hundreds of layers of diamond nanotubes, the strongest, sturdiest polymers known to man. A South Korean company manufactures them for space programs around the world. Every ten yards of cable costs over a million dollars."

"Each one has to be at least thirty yards in length," the Doctor reasoned, trying to calculate the cost in his head. "That means the cables had to cost—"

"A lot of money," Pinchole interrupted. "They are completely vital to the operation. Without them, we would have no hope of transferring and storing the energy until the plant is built."

Pinchole scurried off to get the operation online and ready to roll. The Doctor meandered around the grounds, not quite believing that his grand plan was so close to fruition. His first act with fully functioning geographical transportation would be to send his highly trained assassins through the Warp, knocking off leaders from the most powerful countries in the world, including the president of the United States. The CEOs of oil, gas, and automotive giants like China National Petroleum, Royal Dutch Shell, Volkswagen, and Toyota would come next. The instability would cause stock prices to nose-dive. Then the Doctor Lennon Hatch Geographical Transportation Company would swoop in and save the financial day.

The beautiful, ornamental carvings on the Sun Temple caught the Doctor's attention. He walked onto a large porch, stepped down a double staircase, and came to a shrine containing a statue of a person at least eight feet tall. Being a bit of a rock hound, he knew the ancient artist had used green chlorite stone of extremely high quality.

"Surya," a deep voice said from behind.

The Doctor turned and saw a large Indian man with a thick mustache and wearing a traditional outfit. "Excuse me?" he said, slightly startled.

"The statue is of Surya, the Hindu Sun God," the man explained. "The temple was built to honor him. Traditionally, Surya is depicted as a red man with four arms and three eyes, riding a chariot drawn by seven horses."

"Fascinating, I'm sure."

"Your face is very red, but I see that you don't have three eyes or four arms. Therefore, you are not a god. Am I correct?

"What the hell are you talking about?"

"In my country, Surya is a compassionate spirit who heals the sick and brings good fortune."

The Doctor felt the port-wine stain on his left cheek flush with irritation. As far as he was concerned, there wasn't a person alive who could frighten him. But the eerie presence of the man standing before him was beginning to do just that.

"This whole area is for authorized personnel only," the Doctor said. "You're not supposed to be here."

"I think it is the other way around," the man said, his eyes intense and penetrating. "You are the one who is not supposed to be here."

The man reached up and rubbed his palm against the sun god's exposed navel. The Doctor felt the ground vibrate underneath his feet. The statue's stone eyes appeared to flicker with life. Two Indian soldiers carrying submachine guns rushed down the double stairs. The man removed his hand from the statue. The tremors stopped, and the statue's eyes returned to a cold, dead stare. The man then sprinted down a long corridor.

"Clear that man out of here!" the Doctor shouted to the soldiers. "And anyone else who doesn't have a security clearance badge."

The soldiers made chase as the Doctor looked toward the sunlight-drenched courtyard. He saw a vaguely familiar face wearing a headscarf and an aqua-green sari. The harried woman looked him right in the eye and then quickly disappeared behind one of the many pillars.

"Stop right there!" the Doctor shouted at her. "Don't I know you from somewhere?"

He climbed the double stairs into the sunshine. He spent the next half hour scouring every inch of the courtyard looking for her, but the woman was long gone.

Chapter Forty-Two
DAISHA

Daisha grabbed Axel's hand, and they scurried along the sun temple's ancient walls. Every inch of stone was a collage of carvings and sculptures—camels, cobras, mythical animals, deities, dancers, exotic birds, royal court scenes, and every other conceivable celebration of life. Daisha and Axel hid behind a hedge and watched Indian soldiers escort a bunch of unhappy-looking tourists through the gate. With the visitors out of the way, a convoy of large trucks rolled into the courtyard.

Axel pointed to a man directing traffic. "That guy with the blue shirt carrying an iPad is Pinchole! The Doctor and his men are here!"

"He must have hired the soldiers for security," Daisha said.

"We have to stay hidden, or they'll kill us for sure."

The boy with hair like a muddy river must die yet still live.

Larraj's words echoed inside Daisha's brain. "What does it mean to die while still live?" she mused.

"It's some kind of oxymoron," Axel answered.

"As far as I'm concerned, the past six months are one giant oxymoron. Let's get moving and figure out what to do next."

They turned the corner and slammed into Jag and a woman wearing an aqua-blue sari. The collision was so hard that Axel and Daisha fell to the ground. The head-scarf covering the woman's head slipped off, revealing partially shaved, spiked blue hair.

"It's the woman from the Monitoring Room!" Axel gasped. "She's with the Doctor!"

Daisha and Axel scrambled to their feet and attempted to run, but Jag blocked their way.

"The man with the red face is pursuing all of us," Jag said. "She is on our side."

"Axel, Daisha!" the woman cried. "It's Megan, your parents' grad assistant! Don't you recognize me?"

Daisha studied the woman carefully. The Megan she remembered had long, black hair parted in the middle and eyes the color of an Alaskan glacier. The hair on this woman was much different, but the eyes were the same icy blue.

"I don't believe you," Axel said.

"After what the Doctor has put us through," Daisha added, "we can't be certain of anything or anybody."

"Can you be certain of this?" Megan pulled out her iPhone, opened the photo app, and handed it over.

When Daisha saw what the picture was, she cupped a hand over her mouth and burst into tears. The photo was from two years ago, when Megan, Axel and his dad, and Daisha and her mother went to Fisherman's Wharf in San Francisco. The four of them had been leaning over a guardrail, pointing toward the sea lions sunning themselves on wooden floats, when Megan had snapped the picture. The sky was cloudless and sunny, and Alcatraz Island loomed in the background.

"I've kept the photo on my phone for a long time," Megan said.

"How...what...why," Daisha stuttered, not quite believing that Megan, a living, breathing connection to her old life, was actually standing here.

"When I figured out what the Doctor did to your mom and dad," Megan told her, "I put on a disguise, invented a whole new persona, and infiltrated their operation."

"You can explain this later," Jag interrupted. "We

must go to the Palm Leaf Library. Soldiers are looking for us."

With a touch of Jag's palm against the carving of Garuda, the library door creaked open and the group rushed inside. Daisha expected to see Larraj floating in midair, but the Nadi reader was nowhere in sight.

"Where's Larraj?" Axel asked. "And what happened to all the shelves full of bundled palm leaves?"

"Gone," Jag said. "He and several of the Sun Temple dancers removed every palm leaf prophecy for safe-keeping and fled to the countryside. We are the only ones left."

"What are we supposed to do now?" Daisha asked.

"Fulfill the destiny of your palm leaf," Jag said.

Daisha paced back and forth, chewing on her thumbnail, deep in thought. "Larraj's reading of our palm leaves is starting to make sense," she said. "The Doctor is obviously the red shadow, and Megan is the cloud that breaks away from his thunderstorm to help us."

"Who is this *Larraj* person, and how am I a cloud that breaks away from a thunderstorm?" Megan asked.

Jag told Megan about the Nadi reader. He explained the prophecies written on palm leaves. How the seven sages saw through time and space into the lives of future generations and about their first foretelling written specifically for Daisha and Axel thousands of years ago.

"The ancient sages even predicted how we must demagnetize the X-Point to defeat the shadow," Axel said.

"The last line of the prophecy says that to accomplish this, a boy with hair like a muddy river must die yet still live," Daisha said. "That muddy-haired boy is obviously Axel."

"I don't know about any prophecy," Megan said. "But those ancient gods, or whatever they were, hit it right on the nose about demagnetizing the X-Point. Without a permanent electron diffusion region, the Doctor can't go through with his plans."

"Then we have to figure out a way to ruin his coming-out party," Axel said.

Megan grabbed a stool from the corner of the room and sat down. "I've spent enough time with the Doctor and Pinchole to know what's going to happen here. Any moment now, Pinchole is going to power up those four extremely powerful satellite dishes and send a signal to the space magnets orbiting the globe. When the magnets capture enough electrons floating in the solar wind, SW techs will transfer them to Earth with lasers. The nuclear magnetic resonance spectrometer and thermoelectric converters in the courtyard will funnel that energy directly through the X-Point."

She gave Jag a sympathetic look. "I'm sorry, but this beautiful place will be the first casualty inflicted by the Doctor Lennon Hatch Geographical Transportation Company. The massive amount of solar energy will turn the stone to dust in short order."

"How are we supposed to demagnetize this sucker?" Axel asked.

"I have no idea," Megan said. "I don't think anyone does."

Daisha suddenly had a flash of insight that nearly knocked her over. Her mind swam back to their meeting with Larraj, his words burning in her memory like bare feet on scorching asphalt.

"I think I know how to destroy the X-Point!" Daisha blurted out. "The boy with hair like a muddy river must die yet still live!"

"Daisha, you better start making sense," Axel said. "The Doctor's about to blow up the temple. We're running out of time."

"Larraj told us that by demagnetizing the temple, we free its soul so the divine energy may return to Swarga—Heaven. Remember?"

Axel stared at her blankly, still not understanding.

Daisha grabbed him by the shoulders. "Don't you get it? You need to go through the X-Point with the GeoPort. That's the only way to demagnetize it!"

Axel shook his head. "Like a human sacrifice? Give me a break. I'm not some young maiden a Mayan priest is about to toss off a cliff to appease the gods."

"This has nothing to do with religious superstition," Megan said. "Daisha is talking about pure, hard-core science. Actually, it makes perfect sense."

A loud, skull-splitting shriek of electrical feedback filled the library. Daisha, Axel, Jag, and Megan covered their ears and winced in pain. A moment later, the feedback was gone, but the walls inside the library still shook.

"What's going on?" Jag asked.

"The satellite dishes are firing," Megan said. "They'll take at least thirty minutes to warm up. That's how long we have until the Doctor destroys the Sun Temple and has the power supply for a global geographical transportation system."

"Tell me more," Axel pressed. "I still don't get it."

"The X-Point's massive amount of energy gives us the ability to dematerialize the elemental composition of the human body to a stream of charged particles. We then use the GeoPort to reconstitute those particles back to human form. We need to do the exact opposite to demagnetize the X-Point."

"So what you're saying is instead of the solar wind surging toward me and my GeoPort via an X-Point and allowing me to transfer to any latitudinal and longitudinal point on Earth, I need to go directly *through* the X-Point with my GeoPort and meet the solar wind head on."

Megan nodded. "Yes. And the GeoPort must be set directly to the sun."

"What are the coordinates for the sun?" Daisha asked.

"Latitude and longitude don't exist in space," Megan explained. "Scientists measure the sun in angles. As in which direction and how high the sun is at any time of day." She pulled out her iPhone. "I have an app that measures the solar position from any place on the planet. From where we stand, the sun's declination in degrees is 21.52. Its solar azimuth is 75.3. The solar elevation is 78.14, and the zenith angle is 0.9786. Those are the numbers you must enter to demagnetize the X-Point."

"It doesn't have to be Axel," Daisha protested.

"Yes, it does," Axel said. "The prophecy says it must be me."

"I don't care what some Nadi reader or the seven sages had to say! I'm not going to let you die!"

"I'm tired of running from this maniac! Either he ends or I end."

There was another screech of eardrum-rupturing feedback followed by stronger tremors. A small crack fissured up one of the library's walls. Dust from crumbling stone rained down in their eyes.

Jag grabbed Daisha's trembling hands. "You must not take the prophecy too literally," he said. "Have you heard the parable of the caged eagle?"

Daisha shook her head, wiping away tears.

"A long time ago there was a man who captured a sea eagle and put it in a cage."

"Was it a sea eagle like Garuda?" Daisha asked.

Jag nodded. "The sea eagle longed to fly, fish, and be free. The bird also had a mate that he missed desperately. After many months of captivity, the bird became so depressed and lonely he wanted to die. One day the man returned home from work and found the bird lying motionless on the floor of the cage, apparently dead. Saddened, the man tossed the bird outside on a trash heap. To the man's astonishment, the sea eagle suddenly sprang to life, spread its wings, and flew back to his mate. You see, to attain freedom the bird *had to die while still live.*"

Axel took out his GeoPort and punched in 21.52, 75.3, 78.14, 0.9786. “Let’s get moving,” he said. “If we all want to live, then it’s time for me to spread my wings and die.”

Chapter Forty-Three
DOCTOR STAIN

Pinchole handed the Doctor a hard hat, safety glasses, and a pair of earmuff-style hearing protectors. “You better put these on, especially the ear protection,” he advised. “When the satellites power up, there will be several rounds of extremely loud feedback that would put any heavy-metal rock band to shame.”

The Doctor slipped everything on as Pinchole signaled to one of the SW techs. With the click of a mouse, the four massive satellite dishes rumbled to life. The ground trembled under their feet. Streams of visible, neon-green electromagnetic waves appeared to fire from the center of the dishes into the atmosphere.

“The dishes are drawing in the cyclotron and magnetohydrodynamic waves that our space magnets have captured from the solar wind,” Pinchole explained. “That immense energy source is the fuel that will power your geographical transportation company."

"Fascinating," the Doctor muttered.

"This is nothing. Just wait and see what happens next. You're going to witness an amazing light show. The spectacle will make the aurora borealis look about as impressive as a lit cigarette in a dark alley."

"The natives will fall to their knees in prayer, thinking the world is about to end."

Pinchole laughed. "The world is about to change for them and the rest of humanity. We are ushering in the dawn of a new age."

"GTA—the Geographical Transportation Age," the Doctor said, and then let the hugeness of the moment wash over him. His name would go down with Leonardo da Vinci, Galileo, Edison, the Wright Brothers, Benjamin Franklin, Grace Hopper, and Alexander Graham Bell as one of the greatest inventors of all time. His wealth and power would make Warren Buffet, Bill Gates, Rupert Murdoch, Michael Dell, Sandy Weill, and other business titans look like roadside beggars. Doctor Lennon Hatch would live forever in the annals of time as the man who owned the world.

Axel Jack flashed in his mind. He hated the kid but had to respect the boy's intelligence and tenacity. After all, breaking out of the locked room and stealing back the GeoPort had taken great ingenuity and guts.

"Where do you think they are now?" the Doctor asked Pinchole over the squeals of feedback.

"If you're talking about Axel and Daisha, I have no idea. When we discovered the permanent X-Point, I lost all interest in their whereabouts."

"But they still have the two GeoPorts."

"It doesn't matter. In a few minutes, those GeoPorts will be about as obsolete as a travel agent."

The air around the temple grew heavy with static electricity, making the Doctor's hair stand on end and the red birthmark on his face pulse with heat. He watched with astonishment as the clouds parted and brilliant streaks of fluorescent green, pink, and scarlet light flashed across the sky. The satellite dishes revved harder, greedily sucking in solar waves while the diamond-lined cables gobbled the energy.

"Keep your eye on the temple's crown!" Pinchole shouted with delight. "Any moment there will be a surge of solar energy shooting right down in the center. That's the mother lode, a cosmological zenith that will make the whole world shudder."

A loud, deafening thunderclap exploded above their heads. The local soldiers who had been guarding the gates dropped their guns and fled in terror. A dazzling, angelic beam of white light exploded from the heavens directly onto the center of temple.

"Spectacular!" the Doctor gasped.

The temple's delicate and ancient stone, exquisitely carved by thousands of artisans over a dozen years, quaked under the intense energy. Fissures wormed their way around the foundation. Huge statues of horses, elephants, and lions toppled under the barrage of solar pressure.

"Everyone make sure your hard hats and safety glasses are on!" Pinchole hollered. "The temple is getting ready to implode!"

The Doctor winced in anticipation of what was about to come. Something strange flashed in the corner of his eye. He squinted through the smoke and blinding light and witnessed one of the statues fly open. A Caucasian boy with long, curly brown hair rushed from the opening and sprinted toward the center of the temple, straight at the massive beam of light.

"It's...it's..." Pinchole blurted out, but the Doctor finished his sentence.

"Axel Jack! What the hell is he doing?"

"I don't know," Pinchole said. "But he's a dead piece of meat if he reaches the light. The intense magnetism will suck him into space."

"Then let him die," the Doctor said and then saw two other people rush from the statue.

"Wow!" Pinchole exclaimed. "That's Daisha! But who's the Indian woman chasing after her?"

The woman was wearing an aqua-blue sari. As she ran, the matching scarf covering her head blew off to reveal spiky blue hair.

"Shoot them!" the Doctor ordered.

"No guns," Pinchole retorted. "The magnetohydrodynamic waves could turn those ricocheting bullets into mini nuclear bombs and kill us all."

Rage washed across the Doctor's enflamed face. He balled his fist and punched Pinchole square in the mouth. The director of Satellite Warp science clutched his jaw and crumpled to his knees.

"You three!" the Doctor ordered, pointing toward his security team. "Shoot them! Now!"

The men wearing black suit jackets and white shirts didn't budge. They just stood there, confused by whom they should listen to, their boss or Pinchole.

"Then I'll kill them myself!" the Doctor screamed. He grabbed a gun from one of his men, whipped off his hearing protectors, and charged into the courtyard.

Chapter Forty-Four

AXEL

Axel felt like he was in the middle of a war zone. The earth trembled, thick electrical smoke filled his lungs, and a blinding beam of light poured from the sky directly into the heart of the temple. The intense, beautiful radiance was his final destination. Where he would destroy the X-Point and stop the Doctor in his tracks.

As he moved closer, the light's magnetic property yanked at him. The round metal buttons on his jacket ripped from their stitches and disappeared into the light. His GeoPort, made from many metal parts, pulled from his right hand. He quickly secured the device with both hands and checked the declination coordinates.

21.52, 75.3, 78.14, 0.9786

If Megan was correct, he would fly through the Warp on the solar wind directly into the heart of the sun.

"Axel!" a voice cried out. "Stop!"

He turned and saw Daisha race out of the palm leaf library. Not far behind was Megan, chasing after her in bare feet and stumbling in the sari.

“Go back!” Axel shouted. “You’re not going to stop me!”

“Please...” Daisha started to say, but the rest of her words were lost under another round of ear-piercing feedback.

Axel turned away and bounded up the stone steps two at a time. His sneaker caught on a crack and he stumbled hard against the vibrating stone. His GeoPort fell from his hands. He attempted to pick it up, but the light quickly snatched the device with its magnetic pull and tugged it just out of reach. The energy then reached its greedy claws into Axel, flipping him backward and dragging him feet first toward its illuminated, hungry mouth.

Two sets of strong fingers snatched his hair, wrenching him hard in the opposite direction.

“Ouch!” Axel squealed.

“Hold on!” Daisha’s voice wailed, gripping Axel’s scalp with all her might. “I’ve got you!” She grabbed his hair and braced her feet against a step to clamp herself in place.

“Let go of me!” he pleaded. “This is the only way to

destroy the Doctor! Go back to Jag before this thing sucks you up too."

"You're not going to destroy anything without a GeoPort. Look."

Axel peered over his shoulder and watched his GeoPort scamper farther from his reach. Just then, the arm of a statue crashed to the ground and shattered into pieces, but its large stone hand remained intact and wedged neatly between the toes of an enormous carved elephant. The GeoPort lodged perfectly in the statue's palm, temporarily halting its advancement to the light.

"Let me go," Axel said. "I think I can reach the GeoPort."

"No," Daisha fired back. "We've lost each other before, and I won't let it happen again."

A woman's scream echoed from behind them. Axel looked back and saw Megan and the Doctor. They were wrestling on the ground. Megan was desperately trying to stop him, but the Doctor was too strong. He flung her aside and aimed a gun at her. Just as he was about to pull the trigger, the magnetic suction ripped the gun from the Doctor's hand and sent it flying away.

Axel felt himself lurch forward. Daisha's feet had given way, and now the powerful magnetic force was dragging both of them closer to the light. Pieces of the temple rained down on them. Axel frantically grabbed a large chunk of stone to stop their progress. He saw that the GeoPort was now within arm's reach. The device was vibrating in the statue's hand. As he reached out for it, a sharp pain sliced through his right hamstring.

"Ahhh!" Axel groaned and then looked over his shoulder. Blood gushed from his leg where the Doctor had plunged a pocketknife into his flesh.

"You're dead!" the Doctor roared at Axel.

Daisha, who was still holding on desperately, contorted her body and kneed the Doctor in the nose. Blood gushed from the man's nostrils, the color mixing perfectly with the large port-wine birthmark on the side of his face.

The Doctor shoved her hard. She lost her grip on Axel's legs and fell aside, clutching the fallen head of a lion statue to keep from slipping away. The Doctor leaped onto Axel. He clamped his good hand around Axel's throat, squeezing with all his might, and used the hard cast on his other hand to deliver a series of skull-thumping blows.

"I've got you now!" the Doctor snarled. "I killed your father, destroyed his good name, and stole his life's work. Now I'm going to crush his only son!"

The Doctor clamped down harder, his thumb jamming into Axel's trachea like a sharp spike. Axel's eyes bugged out. Stars danced in front of his face. He was choking to death. He saw Daisha leap into action. She rolled past him like a tumbleweed, snatched the GeoPort from the statue's hand, and swirled off toward the light.

"Da...Da," Axel gagged, and then felt the Doctor's hand release its death grip. Axel gasped as a gush of lifesaving air filled his lungs.

"My god," the Doctor muttered, his eyes wide with shock.

Axel watched Daisha plunge headfirst into the mystical effervescence. A look of fear and panic washed across her face. He heard her shout *I love you* as a kaleidoscopic of colors exploded over the Sun Temple.

"Daisha!" Axel cried.

Daisha surged upward, sweeping away into the vortex of solar wind.

The magnetic pull that had tried so violently to swallow Axel whole was suddenly gone. He pushed away from the Doctor and watched as the light in the center of the temple turned hellish red. The four powerful satellite dishes surrounding the perimeter exploded into a million pieces. The Doctor's other equipment—resonance spectrometer, x-ray lasers, and battery trucks connected by long cables—burst into the flames. Plumes of thick black smoke blotted out the sun.

Axel sat up on his knees and quickly surveyed the surroundings. The temple had sustained damage, but it was still in one piece. In the distance, he saw six helicopters flying in their direction. Racing down the road leading to the temple were trucks, jeeps, and other vehicles with the crossed sword insignia of the Indian Army.

The Doctor let out a labored yet maniacal laugh. "Don't think for a second this is over. I'm always on the winning side. Soon, one of my men is going to feed you to the crocodiles."

Megan and Jag bounded up the steps and helped Axel up.

"The explosions have alerted the authorities," Jag said. "Indian Special Forces will be here any minute. We have to get you to safety."

They carried Axel toward the Sun Temple's Gathering Hall.

Thick smoke filled Axel's lungs. Helicopter wings buzzed in his ears like giant, prehistoric mosquitoes. His thoughts raced with questions. Where was Daisha?

Did he really just witness her fly into the sky? If she was dead, why did her life have to end like this?

A battle raged inside Axel's soul. His heart cried out for the answers to his questions, but his logical brain was too afraid of hearing the truth. Jag pressed his palm against the carving of Garuda, and the secret door slowly creaked open.

"She's the only thing I have left in the world," Axel whispered, tears flooding the corner of his eyes.

"What did you say?" Megan asked through the clamor of military vehicles.

Axel didn't respond. He lowered his head, realizing with great anguish that he had fulfilled his palm leaf prophecy. Without Daisha, he was dead inside. Yet, he was still alive.

Chapter Forty-Five

DAISHA

Daisha soared at supersonic speed through the Warp. An illuminated light show exploded before her eyes in a collage of images and colors. The history of humankind played out like an IMAX movie as she whizzed at the speed of light.

She watched primates stand erect for the first time and take tentative steps on the African savanna. A photographic journal of ancient man taming fire and using stone tools to hunt and scrape hides flashed all around her. Another glimpse showed the world's oceans rising, cutting off England from the rest of Europe, and drowning the Bering Strait land bridge that humans had used to cross into North America.

Man's ingenuity was in full display as the time capsule showed people pushing plows and domesticating wild sheep and cows. She saw the birth of Buddha,

Jesus, Mohammed, Hippocrates, Crazy Horse, and Gandhi. Michelangelo lying on his back while painting the Sistine Chapel and his first chisel marks into a hunk of marble that would eventually become *David*. Her body tingled with awe as she witnessed the creation of the Konanavlah Sun Temple by thousands of workers.

Then a more recent image exploded into view, making Daisha's heart hurt and eyes well with tears. She saw Axel sprawled bloody and wounded on the temple's stone porch. The Doctor had his grubby hands clamped tightly around her best friend's neck. Would he live or die? The horrible question tumbled through her thoughts as she flew directly toward the sun, just as Megan had explained back in the palm leaf library.

Or was it the sun?

The bright white light gleamed gloriously in the distance. The radiance was gentle, calm, loving, serene, and not at all blistering or blinding like staring directly into the sun. The light equaled peace. She wanted to plunge into its depths and bathe in the beauty forever.

Then, like the final act of a Broadway play, a velvet curtain dropped between her and the light. Everything went black. Daisha spiraled downward through an empty void, a skydiver without a parachute. An extreme rush of hot wind blasted her face. Her eardrums popped from the intense pressure. As she reached terminal velocity, unbearable feelings of loneliness and despair clawed at her heart.

Blurry images began to take shape below Daisha's feet. Landing was imminent. She twisted her body parallel to the ground. A cushion of air enveloped her seconds before impact, softening the landing as she fell onto the moist, sandy ground.

Her eyes snapped open. She gagged and dry heaved, her head throbbing. The beautiful light was gone, replaced by utter darkness save for a street lamp a few yards away. City sounds filled her ears—car horns, truck engines, doors slams, garbled voices in the distance.

She sat up and saw a familiar sight in the dim light—Centennial Fountain outside the Green Library at Stanford University. Tears leaked from her eyes. She and Axel had played here as small children. She remembered the whispering gallery and how they could hear each other's every word even though they were far apart.

Daisha walked over and pressed her cheek against its stone surface. "Axel," she said. "Are you there?"

Silence.

"Axel," she repeated a little louder. "Are you there?"

She had just given up hope for a response when an

abrupt blast burst into her ears from the other side of the fountain. The sound wasn't Axel's voice, but the loud bark of a dog. The dog barked again, followed by two deep sniffs.

"No way," Daisha said. "Boris. Is it you, boy?"

The sound of sharp claws on cement and excited yips echoed around the gallery. A moment later, a big black-and-white dog with a curled tail and violet eyes leaped onto her. Daisha hugged Boris as he frantically licked her face. After their slobbery reunion, Boris nuzzled his nose into the front pocket of Daisha's pants. He licked and chewed at the fabric until Daisha pushed him away.

"That tickles," she said. "What do you want?"

Boris barked and then pawed more at her pants. Daisha wormed her fingers into the pocket the dog was so obsessed with and pulled out a blue handkerchief. The one she had found on the ground after Warping to India.

"Is this what's driving you crazy?"

The dog opened his jaws and snatched the hankie out of her hand. He trotted a few yards away, dropped the prize on the ground, and gave the fabric a thorough sniff.

Daisha walked over and stroked Boris's head. "That's Axel's handkerchief," she said, a hint of sorrow in her voice.

Boris woofed, stood on his hind legs, and turned an enthusiastic pirouette. He then took off out of the science garden. His curved tail was wagging a million miles an hour, nose to the ground. That's when Daisha realized what the dog was doing.

"Good boy!" Daisha shouted. "Let's go get him!"

The tiniest twinkle of hope stirred in her heart. She and Boris had found each other, and now it was time for both of them to find Axel.

LOOK FOR THE NEXT BOOK IN THE

SECRETS of the X-POINT

SERIES

COMING SOON

GARY UREY is the author of the Super Schnoz series, which *Kirkus Reviews* called in its starred review "a winner, especially for reluctant readers." Gary is a graduate of the American Academy of Dramatic Arts in New York City where he has portrayed everything from a Shakespearean messenger to a mime trapped in a box on the subway. He puts his professional theater training to good use every time he sits down to write stories for kids.